THE JOURNEY TO MARS

Mars

This is the story of one man's dreams of Mars.

No one knows who he is or where he comes from.
One day, he received a gift that could change everything on
Earth!

Janne OB Larsson (Jan Larsson)

Janne OB Larsson

The Journey to Mars

The Revelation

© 2024 Janne OB Larsson
Illustration: Janne OB Larsson
Publisher: BoD • Books on Demand, Stockholm, Sweden
Print: Libri Plureos GmbH, Hamburg, Tyskland
ISBN: 978-91-8080-097-6

The Journey to Mars

He was on his way to collect the mail from the mailbox. It wasn't far, about 50 meters. The temperature was 25 degrees below zero, and it was a clear winter day somewhere in Norrbotten. The spruce trees were covered in snow, and the sound of his footsteps echoed through the crisp air as he walked. He was an ordinary person, with no higher education, but over the years, he had learned how to tinker with computers and had become quite skilled with electronics.

Halfway to the mailbox, he was struck by an intense headache. He saw flashes of light and a sharp glow in front of his eyes. He stopped in his tracks, and slowly, the pain began to subside. The whole experience lasted maybe a minute, no more. When it was over, he felt a strange sensation—like a fog had lifted from his mind, and everything suddenly became clearer. He resumed his walk, retrieved the mail, and headed back home.

The next day, he sat at the kitchen table, eating breakfast. In front of him was a notebook that he had absentmindedly started doodling in. After a while, he noticed something odd—he had scribbled down several formulas and drawn a diagram. He glanced at the equations, and to his surprise, he understood what they meant.

"Strange," he muttered to himself. "I've never seen these before."

After a moment, he realized that the notes were a blueprint for an electronic machine that he was somehow destined to build. Could this be connected to the strange experience he had on his way to the mailbox? He wasn't sure, but he decided to press forward.

He began listing the components he would need to construct the machine. Hundreds of different diodes, capacitors, and special electronic parts would be required. He searched online for suppliers, adding the components to his cart. But when he saw the total cost, he realized it would be far too expensive to buy everything at once. He decided to purchase the parts gradually, a little at a time.

Over the course of three months, he continued to acquire the necessary materials, slowly building his project. Various metal constructions and converters were also needed. Once he had assembled everything, created circuit boards, soldered the components, and connected the system to a computer, he realized that programming would be required—something he had never done before.

"All of this is incredibly strange," he thought to himself. "I'm designing and programming something I had no prior knowledge of. It feels as though someone—or something—is guiding my actions, helping me understand how everything is supposed to work! But I don't feel afraid; rather, I'm excited to see where this will lead."

He proceeded to mount a camera onto a frame that was 10 cm wide and measured 3 by 2 meters, standing vertically like a large window. Along the inside of the frame, he installed power capacitors, phase shifters, and frequency magnet amplifiers at regular intervals. All of this would be powered by a 380-volt three-phase current. The power distribution would be controlled by the software on the computer.

TIME TO RUN A TEST

The day of the test arrived, and all preparations were complete. The equipment had been supplemented with protective clothing to shield against radiation, as well as oxygen tanks for breathing. All of the equipment, except for the computer, had been installed in a well-insulated room. The room was equipped with an airlock to allow entry and exit, and there was a thick glass window to observe the frame inside.

He connected the electricity, and the electronic circuits began to blink. Everything seemed to be functioning as expected. The computer was ready, waiting for the coordinates of the location to be explored. He entered the longitude and latitude, and the screen displayed:

"All systems OK. Start search? Press ENTER."

He pressed the key, and inside the frame, an image appeared—a grassy lawn with a red ball. Using a joystick, he controlled the view and zoomed in on the ball for a close-up.

He entered the airlock, closed the first door, and then opened the second to step into the room. Carefully, he shut the doors behind him. Taking a grabber tool mounted on a long rod, he slowly extended it towards the window. As the gripping end reached the window, it passed through and became enveloped by the image. He extended the tool further, grabbed the ball, and pulled it back into the room. When the tool and the ball returned, the image vanished, now without the ball.

He had successfully retrieved an object remotely, even though there were miles between his location and the place where the ball had been. Everything had worked as planned. A sort of wormhole had formed, and the distance to the coordinates no longer mattered. He took the ball, exited the room, and closed the doors securely behind him. Then, he examined the ball to see if its material had changed or if there were any traces of radiation.

The machine could indeed transport material from one location to his building. Once he shut down the program, the outer window disappeared, and the wall was solid once again. After the successful experiment, he sat down, satisfied, and began planning the next steps for the machine's use.

The following day, he would conduct a much, much bigger test.

He reviewed his notes with the coordinates he was going to use: Longitude, Latitude: 77.40131021°, 18.45143045°.

These coordinates did not point to any place on Earth, but to Mars—specifically, to the location where samples number 17 and 18, which the Perseverance Rover had placed on the ground, were waiting for a future mission to collect them. He had gathered all the information from NASA's website about the project, where they had marked the rover's path and the locations where the samples had been drilled. NASA planned to send a Mars lander to retrieve the samples and then transport them to Earth using a rocket. This project would cost billions in rockets, fuel, and manpower.

"I have a plan to use the machine to connect and retrieve those two samples, then deliver them to NASA without them knowing anything about the invention," he thought. "I must protect the machine so that it doesn't fall into the wrong hands and get used for malicious purposes."

He realized how dangerous it would be if the construction of the machine became public knowledge. However, he had built in a safety feature that ensured the machine couldn't function unless he personally activated the software or equipment. There was also a self-destruct mechanism that would trigger if the machine didn't register his vital signs.

If the machine worked as he envisioned, a new universe of possibilities would open up. Planets could be explored, no matter the distance, as long as one had the exact coordinates.

TO MARS

The following day, he began preparing everything needed for the connection, including protective gear and an oxygen mask. He couldn't predict what might happen if the machine worked. Would Mars' atmosphere and lower pressure seep into the room? How would the window to a world without oxygen react— would it hold? There were many factors he couldn't foresee. To be safe, he constructed a pressure equalizer so that the pressure in the machine room wouldn't become too high.

Once everything was in place, he activated all functions and input the coordinates into the computer, along with the precise location of Mars relative to Earth. After pressing ENTER, it took a bit longer than usual for anything to happen, but eventually, a window appeared, like a screen within the frame. Outside, a reddish desert, colored by Mars' sand, came into view.

As he gazed at the sand and the pale sun shining in the sky, it struck him that he was the first human to truly see this environment. It felt grand, almost surreal. He saw rocks of various sizes and shapes, and carefully took hold of the joystick to slowly pan the camera to the right. The same formations of sand and rock stretched out before him. As he turned further, something caught his attention: two tracks in the sand, clearly left by the rover that had driven there earlier.

He followed the tracks but saw nothing unusual at first. He turned the camera 180 degrees to look in the opposite direction. After a while, he spotted something glinting next to the tracks. Curiously, he zoomed in and saw two small containers, about 30

centimeters long and a few centimeters thick. Bingo! These were
what he had been searching for.

It was time to act. He donned the protective gear and gas mask
and stepped into the room. Carefully, he checked that the doors
were securely closed before taking the rod with the grabber
attached. Slowly, he moved the rod toward the window,
watching as the grabber passed through the image, now
enveloped by Mars' landscape. With great precision, he opened
the grabber, clamped onto the first tube, and slowly pulled the
rod back into the room.

He placed the first tube into a lead box with a tightly sealed lid,
then repeated the process to retrieve the second tube. Both tubes
were now safely stored in separate lead boxes. He then used a
measuring instrument to check for any radiation emanating from
the boxes. To his relief, he detected no radiation or other
anomalies.

What had fascinated him the most was that the "window"—the
strange interface between the two worlds—had worked
flawlessly. It completely enveloped the rod and the tubes
without allowing any part of Mars' atmosphere or pressure to
enter the room. The surface of the image remained stable, with
no distortion in any direction. The large pressure difference
between Mars and his room had not affected the window or
anything else.

With a deep sigh, he finally released the tension that had been
building up. He hadn't even realized his pulse had spiked to at
least 180 beats per minute. Inside, he was elated by the
success—everything had gone according to plan.

After leaving the room, he shut down the machine via the computer, removed his protective gear and oxygen mask, and performed another check for radiation on the clothing. No readings there either. He restored the room's pressure to normal and felt a sense of satisfaction that everything had gone so smoothly.

THE DELIVERY

He continued with the next part of his plan: finding a way to hand over the tubes without revealing himself or their origin. NASA would get the first tube, but it had to be done in a way that made them take it seriously without risking contamination during examination. The plan was to use the machine to deliver the tube to a place with sufficient resources to analyze it, and for NASA to realize that it was an authentic sample from Mars.

All the information about NASA's Mars project was available online. They had never had any reason to keep it secret—quite the opposite, they wanted to showcase their technical skill and position at the forefront of global research. Online, there were detailed records of the coordinates where the tubes had been left on Mars, how the organization was structured, and who was responsible for the various parts of the project. There were also pictures and information about the research station, along with demonstrations for students who wanted to see all the parts of the project.

He studied all the information carefully and decided where he would leave one of the lead boxes. He wrote an accompanying letter explaining what the lead box contained and how important it was to open it in an absolutely sterile laboratory. Everything was meticulously planned: no fingerprints, no traces of DNA, or anything else that could reveal his identity. It would be exciting to see whether NASA decided to go public with the discovery or if it would remain secret for a long time.

"No, they'll probably stay silent for a long time, with a lot of nervousness within the organization," he thought with satisfaction. He was convinced that they would realize the tube was genuine and that the drilled samples were extraterrestrial.

After checking the location of the lab and its coordinates, he attached a note to the lead box's lid: "It is of utmost importance that you examine the contents of this box in a sterile lab to avoid contamination. I will return with more samples once you have confirmed the authenticity of this Mars sample. According to my tests, there is nothing dangerous in the tube, but you should be cautious. If you confirm its authenticity, announce a breakthrough on your website—then I will return!"

Late at night, in the middle of the night in the U.S., he started the machine and programmed the coordinates for the lab. Just to be safe, he had also installed a stronger light, in case it was too dark in the room, and a video camera to record the entire process. He pressed ENTER and waited.

The screen flickered to life, showing a dimly lit room. He looked around and saw the glass window and protective arms used to examine samples. He maneuvered the gripping arm, placed the box on a table, and left a copy of the message on the other side of the glass where someone could easily see it. To draw attention to the box, he pressed a button that triggered an alarm in the room. Then he disconnected the machine and shut off the power.

"Now it's just a waiting game," he thought.

The next day, at NASA's lab department, an alarm went off. A guard received a warning on the screen and immediately notified

16

security personnel, who rushed to the scene. When they arrived, the lab was empty, but the alarm was still blaring. They inspected the room but couldn't see anything unusual—no computers or lights were on. Following protocol, they contacted the research leader, Walter Collings. Having been woken up in the middle of the night, Collings groggily answered:

"Yes, this is Collings. What's going on?"

"There's been an alarm in the lab," the guard replied, describing the situation. Collings asked them to stay at the room, saying he would come as soon as possible.

Twenty minutes later, Collings arrived, looked around, and entered the room. On the bench by the glass window was a lead box, and on top of it, a note. He read the note several times, pondering what to do.

"A Mars sample? Is this a joke?"

Collings ordered the guards to contact Brian Adams, head of the geology department for the Mars project. When Adams arrived, noticeably tired and out of breath, Collings showed him the box and asked him to read the note. Adams read it, and his confusion deepened with each reading.

"Where did this come from?" Adams asked.

"No idea," Collings replied. "It was here when we arrived. The alarm button was pressed manually, but security footage shows no one in the room or hallways."

"We need to examine this box," Adams said. "We can use the remote controls and robotic hands behind the glass. If anything happens, we'll be at a safe distance."

"Good, do it," Collings responded.

The guards were ordered to remain outside and keep quiet about what they had seen. Adams activated the remote controls and adjusted the camera toward the bench. Using the robotic hands, he carefully lifted the box's lid. To their surprise, inside was a tube that looked exactly like the ones NASA had sent to Mars. Adams gently picked up the tube, but the box was otherwise empty. He placed the tube back and moved the robotic hands away from the table.

"It seems safe to continue the examination from inside the room," Adams said.

They entered the lab, and Adams placed his arms into the protective sleeves to pick up the tube. Upon closer inspection, he confirmed that it looked exactly like the tubes NASA had sent to Mars. He placed it into a spectrometer for an initial analysis. The results showed that the contents consisted of reddish sand and gravel, clearly from Mars.

"This is definitely not terrestrial material," Adams said. "And it's our tube. We need to run more tests, but I'm sure it's authentic."

Collings replied: "This must be kept secret. We need to figure out how it ended up here."

Adams agreed that only a few scientists should be informed about this. Meanwhile, Collings planned to notify NASA's leadership.

"Can you retrieve the video recording and the results from the initial tests?" Collings asked.

In the afternoon, NASA's leadership gathered for a meeting. They had been informed of a potential breakthrough in the Mars project. When Collings arrived, noticeably excited, the chairman gave him the floor. Collings recounted the morning's events and the initial test results. He showed the video recording of the box's opening and the examination of the tube.

The leadership was shocked and asked how this could have happened. Collings explained that they had no idea and that there were no traces of fingerprints or DNA on either the tube or the box—they were clinically clean.

"OK," the chairman said. "Continue investigating the tube, and when you're completely sure, you can announce that we've made progress with analyzing the Mars samples."

NASA'S BREAKTHROUGH

The man occasionally visited NASA's website. It took several weeks before NASA announced that they had made progress in their efforts to retrieve the sample tubes from Mars. They gave no details about the breakthrough, only mentioning that it was in the early stages and that they would provide more information as soon as possible. He began preparing for the next step in his contact with NASA, which would occur at night, U.S. time, when he planned to deliver the second lead box.

While waiting, the man experimented with his machine. He set the coordinates to his own backyard to test the machine's functionality. When the image of the backyard appeared, he went outside to see how it looked from the outside. He saw nothing. He then tried sticking out a rod a few centimeters through a window and went back outside to observe. Sure enough, he could see the tip of the rod, but to an outsider, it would barely be noticeable—it looked like a tiny speck, something the wind could have easily blown in. This was exactly what he had expected.

At night, U.S. time, he connected the machine again to the same coordinates at NASA as before. The light was brighter this time. Using the joystick, he surveyed the room and saw a person sitting on guard. The person looked tired and was just staring straight ahead. The man changed direction and looked at the spot where he had left the first lead box. Now there was a piece of paper with large text:

"We don't know how the box ended up here, but if you or your group wish to contact us, we are very interested in dialogue. There is no doubt that it is our sample, and we are both surprised and alarmed by how someone could have gotten hold of our tube. There were no machines or other traces nearby, and we have constant satellite monitoring over Mars. We have had to maintain full alert here at the site. Please contact us! You can reach us via secure email: nasamars@nasa.gov."

The man put on gloves and wrote a new message on a clean piece of paper, leaving no fingerprints:

"I have built a machine that allows me to transport myself anywhere without leaving my building, no matter the distance. It's a type of wormhole that makes invisible movement possible. No traces are left where I travel, so you won't know when I'm there. I can see the guard sitting by the door. As you understand, I can't reveal the technology, as it would upset the balance of power on Earth. If anything happens to me, the technology will disappear and can never be recreated. However, I can offer you services in the future, provided they don't involve war or espionage. My machine is meant to benefit all humanity. Once we reach an agreement, I will need some capital. I will contact you through your email address. If you try to track me, I will notice, and you'll never hear from me again."

He zoomed in and carefully pushed out his message on top of NASA's paper. The guard noticed nothing, as the doorframe blocked the view. The man then took the second lead box and placed it quietly in the room. The guard remained oblivious. He disconnected the machine and called it a day before heading to bed.

The next day, the man began researching secure methods for sending emails and making money transfers without being traced. By using encrypted keys and computer connections through multiple servers in different countries, he could protect his identity. He opened an account in Switzerland that would allow discreet transfers to his Swedish bank.

The following morning, Collings went to the lab and discovered another lead box. When he read the note in the room, he was shocked.

"It can't be possible for someone to travel through time and space," he thought, despite Einstein's speculation on the subject in his theory of relativity.

He contacted NASA's chairman and informed him that yet another lead box had appeared and that the person who left it claimed to possess seemingly impossible technology. Once again, Collings stood before the board and read the message. Several board members shook their heads.

"This can't be true," they said.

Collings replied, "There's no other explanation, even though all the research indicates it's impossible. We're not aware of any developments in this field, and it's unlikely we wouldn't know if such research existed."

The chairman suggested contacting the president, as this could be one of the greatest discoveries ever, if indeed traveling through wormholes was possible.

"We can't ruin this opportunity," the chairman said. "Let's not involve the FBI. We'll wait for the president's decision."

The board unanimously agreed to follow the chairman's suggestion. The chairman contacted the president and presented all the details. He proposed not involving the FBI to avoid risking the collaboration with the man. The hope was to gain access to the technology, which could eventually change the world.

The president gave the green light and asked them to handle the situation with the utmost confidentiality.

The man sent an email to nasamars@nasa.gov through the secure channels he had previously used. He asked how they viewed the situation and if they had seen the second lead box.

"Yes, we've seen your message and the second tube. The research results from these are very important and will provide us with new insights into Mars's history. Naturally, we can agree on an exchange of services, and we are ready to pay a reasonable amount. Both you and we know that if we can obtain all the sample tubes, we'll save billions. We have informed President Biden, and we have the go-ahead to collaborate without any attempts at espionage against you. Of course, we're interested in your machine, which would be invaluable in finding habitable planets. If you provide us with a bank account, we are prepared to deposit one million dollars once we agree on obtaining the remaining tubes from the Perseverance Rover. Once we reach an agreement, we will program the rover to release the tubes."

He responded, stating that he could retrieve the tubes if NASA provided him with the Mars coordinates where they would leave them. He also wrote that payment could be discussed once all the tubes had been delivered. The reply came quickly:

"We will get back to you in a few days. Programming the rover takes time since we must ensure it releases the tubes without the risk of running them over."

By this point, the man was confident that NASA wouldn't risk missing the chance to acquire the valuable samples that would revolutionize Mars research.

While waiting for the next email, he delved into improving the machine and considered how to build a larger version that could transport bigger machines and construction materials. This would be necessary if scientists wanted to build houses on Mars using 3D technology, as it would require more space. He also realized the technology could be used to explore exoplanets discovered by the Hubble and James Webb telescopes. This could potentially lead to the discovery of habitable planets, or even life. He also began wondering where he had gained all the knowledge and drive to build the machine. It couldn't just be a coincidence—he was convinced that some form of extraterrestrial intelligence had influenced his mind. Perhaps it was their intention for him to find them on his own terms. For now, it was only speculation.

Two weeks later, he received a new email from NASA:

"We have successfully retrieved the tubes from the rover and placed them in a row between its tracks. They are located at Mars coordinates 77.40855217°, 18.45559291°."

He went to the machine room, started the machine and computer, programmed the coordinates, and pressed ENTER. Once again, a window opened, showing Mars's red sand. He turned the window to the right and saw the rover's tracks. A bit further ahead, he spotted the rover, and when he zoomed in, he saw the tubes lying on the ground between the tracks. He put on protective gear and an oxygen mask and entered the room. Using the rod, he picked up one tube at a time and placed them in boxes. When he was done, he had 16 boxes on the table. After turning off the machine, he tested for any radiation, but it was safe. He removed the protective gear and began preparing the delivery to NASA.

He connected the machine to the same coordinates as before. When the window opened, he saw the familiar lab, but it was brighter than before. He zoomed around the room and discovered a small camera in a corner. Irritated, he immediately shut off the machine and wrote an email to NASA:

"You broke our agreement. You didn't think I'd notice the camera you installed in the room. There will be no delivery of the 16 tubes! How could you be so foolish to risk research worth millions of dollars for nothing?"

The reply came quickly:

"We sincerely apologize. The security chief, who was not informed of our agreement, installed the camera after the alarm was triggered the first time you were in our lab. The camera was aimed at the door and hasn't recorded any images from your latest entry. We will immediately remove the camera and have instructed the security chief that no cameras are allowed in the lab, as such footage poses a security risk. Once again, we apologize and hope you can accept this explanation. No one will be near the lab at night, we promise."

Although the apology seemed credible, he let NASA sweat for a while and didn't respond immediately. After a few days, he connected to NASA again. When the window opened, he saw that the camera had indeed been removed, and the room was only dimly lit. He took one box at a time and placed them on the lab table. Once all 16 boxes were in place, he turned off the machine.

The next day, he received an email from NASA:

"Thank you for trusting us! We would like to pay for your services. If you give us an account number, we will make a deposit as soon as possible. We are prepared to pay the amount we previously discussed."

He replied and wrote: "The amount you previously suggested will be sufficient." He provided the account number for his Swiss bank account and concluded with: "I'll get back to you later if you want to plan additional projects where you need assistance. I'm thinking you might want to explore an exoplanet, and we can discuss the necessary conditions regarding pressure, radiation, altitude, oxygen, and so on. You already know quite a bit through the James Webb Telescope, so you can start planning and gathering facts about potential risks."

After this, he once again began contemplating how he could improve the machine. He decided to build a steel structure to seal against the frame and install cameras to monitor the area between the plate and the frame window. He realized he needed various tools to measure toxic gases, acids, radiation, and other hazards. The entire room would be reinforced and made bombproof with proper ventilation. Additionally, an airlock would be installed to eliminate toxic substances when leaving the room. He also realized that he needed spacesuits as secure as those used by NASA, which could be a challenge to acquire. But with the right resources, it could be arranged – everything was a matter of money.

PAYMENT FOR SERVICES

A few days later, he received confirmation that the funds had been deposited into the account. He transferred 400,000 SEK to his personal account and began to consider how he would acquire materials for the machine room update. He realized it would be difficult to buy parts on the open market without attracting attention. One solution would be to get help from NASA, but he also thought that he could use his machine to fetch the materials himself.

He sent an email to NASA, asking if they could provide equipment such as space suits, measuring instruments, and other gear suitable for unknown environments. He requested that the materials be placed in the lab so he could retrieve them via the machine. Additionally, he asked if they had any specific exoplanets they wanted to investigate, and if so, if they could provide him with coordinates and directions.

After further consideration, he realized it would be too risky to attempt to connect to an unknown location from his house. He needed more advanced tools to adjust for the rotation of planets and Earth. He decided to quickly contact NASA again.

In his new email, he asked NASA to disregard the recent request for materials and informed them that he was considering a different approach. He promised to provide them with an update soon. The response from NASA came shortly:

"We understand and will await further instructions. We are ready to assist with measuring equipment and other materials when needed."

While sitting at his kitchen table drinking coffee, he considered various paths forward. All options involved some form of collaboration with NASA. He realized that his technical expertise was too valuable to continue experimenting alone. He reprogrammed the machine with several security layers, requiring unique keys and codes to start it. If incorrect codes were used, all programming would be erased, rendering the machine unusable. This way, he felt secure in operating the machine even with others present.

Once he had decided how to proceed, he wrote a message to NASA:

"I have been thinking and would like to propose a collaboration where I can lead the work in one of your facilities to build a larger and more powerful version of the machine. The project would require the highest security, and I will implement barriers that make it impossible to use the machine without me or to connect anywhere other than outside Earth. The machine will be able to transport materials to research targets, which would be a tremendous advancement for science. My hope is that we can find life on other planets, but I have one condition: the project must be international. If not, I will contact other countries to ensure the technology is shared globally. This is a project that must benefit all of humanity.

If you are interested, appoint someone with decision-making authority and get back to me."

A few hours later, NASA's response arrived:

"Of course, we can do this. We have received approval for the necessary expenses, and we have a large facility available for the construction. We understand your security requirements and will ensure that your invention is protected against misuse. The project's significance also makes international collaboration an advantage. It could help reduce conflicts and create new opportunities. We look forward to starting.

I, Walter Collings, have been appointed to lead the project and will stay in contact with you."

Following this, he began sketching a design for the machine's frame components, excluding details about the electronic components. He sent measurements and instructions to Collings so that NASA could begin installation. Since NASA already had plans to establish a Mars base, he asked them to prepare with radiation-proof housing and power supply via solar panels, but with the added feature that his machine would allow for the delivery of large quantities of material through an opening four by five meters, with a ramp for transporting machines and building materials.

He knew it would take time to prepare and build. However, NASA had the resources, and without the need to build spacecraft, the project would progress faster. It would still take at least six months before the framework was ready to install the electronic systems.

THE LARGER MACHINE

He prepared to order the components and sensors needed for a much larger machine. He also tested how long he could maintain a connection to Mars before the wormhole became unstable. He found that after four hours, the connection began to flicker slightly. He decided that a maximum opening of three hours per session would provide a sufficient margin.

He kept in regular contact with Collins via email for additional instructions as the project progressed. He etched the circuit boards that would be used and the special connectors required for the machine to function. He also created a backup of the software to be installed on a more powerful computer.

It had been a hectic time for him, but now he could relax and live normally. He didn't have much of a social life, which was convenient because no one questioned what he was doing.

He also conducted a test by connecting to the back of his house, which had no visibility due to a high hedge and forest behind it. He did as he had done before and extended a piece of the rod into the right image panel of the machine. Then he went to the back and saw the tip protruding slightly. He moved his hand in the area beside the tip and carefully pushed it in. His hand disappeared into and out of the machine room. He felt nothing, and it was easy to get inside.

He tried to figure out why nothing from Mars came through, given the difference in atmospheric pressure, and why nothing passed through. It seemed that a solid object was required to open the window. He conducted several experiments under different conditions and learned the limits. He sprayed water beside the rod's tip at various pressures, but the water just bounced off the opening, and nothing entered the room. Now he knew that one could pass both ways when the machine was connected!

One day, while reading the newspaper about the war in Ukraine, he had a wild idea. He pondered it and decided to investigate. He opened a history book and looked at blueprints of the Kremlin palaces in Moscow to see where the various rooms were located. It was easy to find the coordinates of the location, and he connected to them. When the machine started, he saw a large, empty hall. He studied where the doors were and noted the distances between them. He disconnected and connected again, this time with adjusted coordinates. A room that looked private appeared. There was another door that stood open, and he moved towards it to take a look inside. Across the room, a guard was sitting on a chair reading a magazine. He estimated the distance to the door and added another two meters. When he connected again, he found himself in a bedroom where a couple was sleeping. He immediately recognized the man as Putin. He shut down the machine and noted the coordinates for the bedroom.

Had he been a different kind of person, he might have seized the opportunity to eliminate Putin, but he knew that wouldn't improve the situation for Ukraine. A new leader would only continue the war. There might be another way. But that would have to wait for another time.

THE JOURNEY TO THE USA

The next day, when he woke up, he packed a suitcase and booked a flight to Stockholm, and from there, a connecting flight to New York City, USA. He drove to Luleå and parked in the long-term parking lot. After passing through security, he bought a sandwich and a large cup of coffee at the café. While he ate, he observed the people passing by; some appeared nervous and stressed, while others seemed like seasoned travelers. He glanced at the information screen and saw that it was time to head to gate 2.

Upon arriving at Arlanda, he had lunch at Sky City and then proceeded to the international terminal to get to the gate for his flight to New York. It was an eight-hour journey, and he spent a significant part of it sleeping, arriving quite rested. He took another flight to Houston. Upon arrival, he checked into a hotel near the Space Center. The next day, he contacted a real estate agent to look at houses relatively close to the NASA facility. They had several properties that were somewhat secluded. He was looking for a slightly larger house with a substantial basement. He bought a house that was a half-hour drive from the NASA center. He signed a contract with a company to install security alarms and manage the exterior. A technician came and installed broadband on the upper floor; he handled the basement installation himself. He measured the coordinates in the basement for future use.

When he returned home from his trip to the USA, he began setting up a connection to the basement of his newly purchased house. He carried in the boxes with equipment, tools, and all the electronic components he had bought. He acquired parts to build a copy of the machine so he could operate it from the basement of the house. The next time he travels to Houston, he plans to assemble the parts and construct a separate room for the machine and the computer.

THE EXTORTION

One night, a few weeks later, he activated the machine with the coordinates from the bedroom in Moscow. When the image appeared, he was lucky; it was only Putin sleeping in the bed. He zoomed in on Putin's face and took a tube connected to a spray can containing a gas that induces sleep, and sprayed it. The gas is not harmful, but inhaling it puts a person to sleep for at least three hours.

He grabbed Putin under the arms, pulled him into the room, placed him on a cot, and restrained him with handcuffs. Knowing that Putin held a black belt in judo, he was careful to be cautious.

After about three hours, Putin began to stir and wake up. When he opened his eyes, he looked around and started shouting a barrage of Russian curses, or so he assumed. The man waited a moment and said in English that Putin should calm down and that he would not be harmed. Putin continued to speak in Russian, and the man repeated the message in English. Eventually, Putin sat quietly and looked at him. He seemed nervous and far from his usual tough demeanor.

The man stood up and walked towards the door. Putin called out, "Wait, stay, explain why I am here against my will." He said this in English this time.

The man turned around and sat in a chair a few meters from Putin. He said: "The whole world wants to punish you for what you are doing to Ukraine, and I could hand you over to The Hague to be prosecuted for crimes against humanity. But I am not going to do that if we can come to an agreement." Putin looked at him with obvious fear.

He asked the man what the agreement would entail. The man replied: "You will order your armies to withdraw from all of Ukraine and publicly apologize for the war, stating that it has gone too far. You will also promise to pay war reparations for the rebuilding of Ukraine."

Putin responded that he would never agree to that. He argued that even if he were harmed or imprisoned, someone else would take over.

The man said he would show Putin something that would make him agree. He started the machine again and connected to Putin's bedroom. Many people were searching the room and seemed worried. The man told Putin that it was pointless to scream; they would neither hear nor see anything. He disconnected the machine, programmed new coordinates, and connected again. This time the image showed Mars with tracks from the Rover and Perseverance further ahead. The man walked up to the image and demonstrated by placing a red ball between the tracks and then retracting the rod. Putin stared, looking very confused.

The man continued: "This machine allows me to control anywhere without being seen. A wormhole forms, and I am the only one who can use it. I have arranged for the USA to have access to the technology if anything happens to me. Imagine what I could do to you and your country. I can place bombs, toxic gas, or anything else you can imagine. I am in contact with NASA and have shown them the technology; we are about to start a research collaboration on space exploration. But I have made it a condition that the machine cannot be used against any location on Earth; only I can do that. I have also stipulated that the research must involve the major countries; otherwise, it will not happen. Right now, NASA is building a facility much larger than this machine. If Russia wants to be part of the project, you need to decide now. Otherwise, I cannot guarantee that we won't strike against your army and leadership."

Putin realized he was in an impossible situation and, after a long silence, said he would agree to the demands if he was granted amnesty for the crimes his army had committed. The man responded that he would make this demand to the USA and other countries.

"I will release you, and if nothing changes within a week, our agreement will no longer be valid. Then, it won't help you to look over your shoulder, as you won't see what's coming!"

Putin agreed to follow the man's instructions. Before Putin could react further, the man sprayed the sleep-inducing gas on him, and Putin immediately slumped over. The man activated the machine and tested it in the first room of the Kremlin. There were no people present. He carried Putin to the window and gently laid him on the floor.

Then the man turned off the machine and went to the kitchen to have a cup of coffee. He hoped he had done the right thing for world peace by not harming him.

WORLD PEACE

On the fourth day afterward, there were major headlines announcing that Russia had withdrawn from Ukraine and even from the Crimean Peninsula. People around the world watched Putin on TV, where he apologized and announced that Russia would fund the reconstruction of Ukraine. All the news stations speculated about why Putin had taken this action and whether he might have fallen ill. It was a joyous day for Ukraine's president, who was interviewed and stated that he was willing to continue discussions with Putin.

The man sent an email to Collings explaining what he had done. He mentioned that Russia would also be included in the project and demanded that the USA work towards granting Putin amnesty. "It is the only way forward," he wrote in the email.

When Collings received the email, he was greatly surprised. It was only then that he realized the immense power of the man's invention. Everything could change in the world, and he now truly understood why the man had been so cautious about letting others control the new technology. There was also a risk that the man might go too far and develop megalomania. Collings informed the board about why Putin had ended the war against Ukraine. The board, in turn, informed the president. The entire balance of power could now be upended! Nevertheless, it was decided to continue with the project, and the president contacted Putin as well as the president of China, proposing a collaboration on the space program. They would also appoint scientists to participate in the project for the benefit of the entire planet. The vision was to use the project to address climate change and overpopulation, with the hope of finding a planet suitable for habitation. First and foremost, the Mars project would serve as a starting point for international cooperation and be used as a base for further research. The president suggested that Putin should receive amnesty.

A month later, the discussions and debates about why Putin had ended the war and surrendered had died down. The news that the USA, China, Russia, India, and Brazil had agreed to collaborate on researching Mars's history and eventually placing scientists there garnered significant attention. It became a major event among leaders in all these countries; instead of a space race, they would now cooperate.

The man received word from Collings that the construction of the new machine hall would be completed in a few days. He replied that he would contact him in three to four days. He booked a flight for the next day from Luleå to Houston. The following day, he drove his car and parked in the long-term parking at Kallax Airport.

SPACE CENTER

The flight to Houston went smoothly without any delays. He went directly to a store, bought the supplies he needed, and then headed to the house. When he arrived, he brewed some coffee and relaxed, feeling a bit tired from the journey. He rested for a while.

The next day, he was fully recovered. He went down to the basement, unpacked the boxes, and began assembling the frame and installing the electronics. He ran a cable down to the basement and connected the broadband to his computer. Then, he ordered a taxi and went to a car dealership, where he bought a used Tesla and an electric charger, which he installed in the garage. He started the computer and wrote an email to Collings:

"I'm in Houston now and planning to come see you tomorrow. My name is Lars Jansson, and I'll need an ID badge to access your site. I expect to drive in with my car and park near the hall, as I'm bringing some equipment with me!"

After a few minutes, Collings replied:

"That's great news, it will be fun to meet. When you arrive at the gate, give them your name, and they'll give you a pass that we can later update with a photo to avoid any issues inside the area. A guard will show you the way to the hall. I'll be there all day. You're welcome."

The next day, he drove his car out of the garage and activated the house alarm via remote control. He set the GPS in the car to the main entrance of the Space Center and drove off. When he arrived at the gate, he showed his driver's license to the guard who approached the car. The guard thanked him, handed back the license, and asked him to follow them to the parking lot outside the hall. He followed the guard, and when they stopped, the guard pointed to a parking spot near the building wall. He parked, locked the car, and followed the guard to a door, which the guard opened. Inside stood a man who extended his hand and said:

"Welcome, I'm Alex Collings. I'll show you around!"

Lars thanked the guard and followed Collings. As they walked through the building, Collings explained the functions of the different rooms and showed where the dining area was located. He informed Lars that the dining area was open from seven in the morning until eight in the evening. They continued down the hallway until they reached the large hall where the frame was placed against the far wall. Collings pointed to the left, at the corner where they stood, to a door with a large window beside it.

"There's a big office you can use. It's equipped with computers, connections, and printers. All the connections are secure from intrusion. There are no cameras or anything that can monitor what you're doing here. You can cover the window with blinds. And that third door over there is my office," Collings said, pointing to the door.

They moved on to the frame, where Collings showed a steel frame that extended from the wall. He explained that it could be closed in front of the frame to prevent anything dangerous from entering the room when connecting. When it was closed, the area was completely airtight between the frame and the hall. There were sensors and various measuring tools, as well as several cameras monitoring the frame. Collings explained that it was set up so that Lars could connect equipment via a cable drum placed inside the steel wall. This would allow for control and reading of the recorded data. He also explained that when Lars was setting up the electronics, he could press a button from his office that would activate a flashing sign on the walls, signaling that the hall needed to be evacuated. A red light outside the door at the entrance to the hall would also light up. Under these conditions, Lars could make the connections without anyone observing him. Collings assured him that no cameras would be active as long as the sign and the red light were on, as per the agreements they had discussed earlier.

Lars thanked him for the tour and suggested they sit in the dining area for some coffee and a chat.

"It was brave of you to talk to Putin. You've really done a good deed for the whole world," Collings said.

"I also wanted to show how dangerous this invention could be if it fell into the wrong hands. That's why I've been so cautious. To protect myself and others, I've taken safety measures that prevent the machine from being started. If anyone tries, it won't work; vital parts will be destroyed," Lars replied.

"In my opinion, you've done the right thing. The technology is frightening. It's important that you also use it responsibly and don't exploit it for personal gain," said Collings.

"What I did with Putin was really an exception so that the Russians could also participate in the project. We cannot allow any single country to control such a technology. I've acquired this knowledge in a strange way! I think I was chosen, and this knowledge was transferred to me. I had a severe headache and saw a blinding light. Why I was chosen, I don't know. My theory is that it comes from some other life form because I've always been interested in space and new technology. I have a strong feeling that I'll get more information about this in some way," Lars explained.

"That's interesting! We've wondered why there hadn't been reports of any significant research in this area before. It's now crucial that you stay safe. If you want, we can arrange protection for you," Collings suggested.

"No, thanks! I don't want any protection. That's why I've been secretive, and it's important that not many people know about me. Have you informed the board about my name?" Lars asked.

"It happened so quickly when you contacted me that I only informed the guard of your name. No one else knows for now," Collings replied.

"I'd appreciate it if not too many people know my name. Here at the facility, I can act as a technician installing equipment. Is that okay with you?" Lars asked.

"Absolutely, we'll make sure that only a small circle of people is aware of the connections and that you're in charge. I've gathered that you're not from around here. When you speak, you seem to be from Scandinavia. Do you have a place to stay here in Houston?" Collings asked.

"I bought a house a bit away from here. The money you transferred helped me arrange housing and a car, among other things," Lars replied.

"Speaking of which, we plan to pay you a consulting fee monthly. We were thinking $50,000 a month. Is that okay, or do you think it's too little?" asked Collings.

"That's more than enough for me, but okay. I'll be purchasing expensive electronics and parts. You have my account information," Lars replied.

Lars began installing the cables that would be connected to the frame and set them up on a very powerful computer he had purchased. The computer was equipped with multiple security locks and a robust firewall when retrieving data from NASA's data system.

The next day, he began installing the electronic components into the frame and connecting the cables to the computer. He had calculated how much power would be required to run the machine since it was many times larger than the previous model. While performing the installations, he ensured no other technicians were in the hall by pressing a button that activated the evacuation signal. He set the coordinates to his house in Sweden and pressed ENTER. The large frame filled with images from his machine room, almost faster than the smaller machine. He walked up to the frame, took a lightweight metal rod, and pushed it through the image; it passed through and was enveloped by the image. He tested closing the outer steel frame and saw on the monitors that the room was clearly visible. He opened the steel frame and turned off the machine, satisfied that everything was working as it should. He deactivated the warning lights, and the technicians could resume their work.

The bridge to the frame had been completed, allowing vehicles to drive through the frame. Lars contacted Collings and informed him that the machine was working and that it was now up to him to decide the next steps.

Collings shared with Lars what they planned to do. First, they would test with a remote-controlled small vehicle that would drive a short distance on Mars' surface to measure the consistency and load-bearing capacity of the sand. He also planned to invite two scientists from each participating country, including India and Sweden.

During the week, scientists from various countries arrived. Once everyone had gathered, Collings assembled them in a conference room and explained the conditions and safety measures. Everyone had to sign confidentiality agreements to protect information about the technology and the upcoming missions. Collings also reviewed what the USA planned to install on Mars, and each representative described their research goals. Collings had previously agreed with each country to share the costs based on the countries' size and economy. For all of them, it would be much cheaper than their own research. Lars was introduced as the coordinator responsible for the connections to Mars and the safety data. Collings emphasized that no one was allowed to touch or stand behind Lars when he operated the machine, but they could communicate if they had specific locations on Mars where they wanted to install something.

After the briefing, everyone went to the hall and stood far away from the frame. Lars connected the computer, set the coordinates to Mars where the Rover was located, and pressed ENTER. When the image appeared, there was a murmur among the scientists. Lars grabbed the joystick and shifted the view to the side so they could see the Rover's tracks. Then he rotated 180 degrees and showed the Rover in place. After a moment, the scientists approached, looking puzzled and amazed at the frame. Lars took the rod he had previously tested, stuck it into the image, and scraped the ground. When he pulled the rod back, the marks on the ground were visible, eliciting another murmur.

Collings spoke: "As you can see, we are now connected to Mars at specific coordinates. It is now possible to access it with the right equipment. Tomorrow, we plan to send in a remote-controlled mini-tractor to measure the consistency and load-bearing capacity of the sand. For each connection, careful planning and preparation are essential, as the window will only be open for a maximum of three hours. Along with the tractor, a strong transmitter will be placed beside it, allowing us to test remote control from Earth."

Lars sat behind the computer and shut down the machine. It became clear that most were quite tense; one could see them exhale in relief.

The next day, everyone gathered in the hall again, and now a smaller, battery-powered front loader with equipment in its scoop had been placed there. When the machine started, a technician with a handheld transmitter carefully drove toward the frame, where the image's bottom edge was right at the ground. The technician slowly drove into the image and continued forward. Lars tilted the image upward slightly, showing the rear of the front loader. The technician steered a bit to the left and tipped the equipment, which slowly slid into the red sand. The technician pressed a button, and a weak light started blinking on the transmitter. A solar panel unfolded to keep the transmitter running and charge the battery.

The technician then backed the machine away a bit and activated the measuring instruments mounted under and along the sides of the tractor. On the monitors next to the frame, various measurements of the sand's consistency and the ground's hardness were displayed. The tractor also had solar panels on its roof for charging, and a pipe on top could remove dust that the wind had deposited on the panels, as well as on the transmitter's solar panel. They managed to connect to the tractor and remotely control it from Earth, though with a delay of at least ten minutes. The cameras on the tractor displayed images in all directions. When Lars shut down the machine, the image disappeared, and Collings confirmed that everything had gone according to plan.

In the following days, equipment was delivered to various locations on Mars. For example, China had a rover almost on the opposite side of Mars, which meant they had daylight at different times on the Martian day.

To make a long story short, many different projects were installed on Mars' surface. Sometimes, sandstorms occurred, and they had to wait until they passed. Earlier plans included building structures using a massive 3D printer with materials from Mars' surface. However, instead, they could now deliver materials from Earth to the printer. Larger machines performed groundwork to ensure that the buildings were securely anchored to Mars' surface. The printer constructed several buildings with walls that shielded against radiation. Inside the large building, partitions were also made for bedrooms for those who would work there. They also developed various vehicles that were radiation-proof and suitable for Mars' surface. Much of the construction was done with the help of robots that installed measuring tools and solar farms to provide enough power to the buildings. Interior materials, like doors and lighting, could be delivered directly into the building when the machine connected to the appropriate coordinates. Several systems ensured the buildings had oxygen and that there were no leaks through security doors.

For safety reasons, a small machine with a frame was installed, which could connect to NASA so that the personnel on Mars could be evacuated in case of an emergency.

Lars programmed the computer so that, with the push of a button, it could connect to the project sites without him needing to be present. But only those locations could be connected to. In another part of the hall, he installed a smaller frame that could be used for transporting personnel to and from Mars. The larger frame would be needed for other projects.

SEARCHING FOR EXOPLANETS

It was time to embark on the most important mission: identifying potentially habitable planets with oxygen, if such planets even existed. Since we couldn't predict the conditions on these various planets, it was crucial to maintain the highest level of security with the steel plate in front of the frame.

The countries that had conducted research and investigations into planets shared their experiences and data on where in the universe there were likely planets worth exploring. The problem was measuring exact coordinates across light-years of distance; no instruments existed that could measure such vast distances with enough precision. The solution was to move telescopes into the Milky Way to measure distances with an accuracy deviating only by a few meters.

The scientists decided that the exoplanet Europa could be a good starting point. As far as we know, it's an ice planet with likely large oceans beneath the surface, but it was deemed uninhabitable for humans. However, it could be worth investigating the sun's nearest neighboring star, Proxima Centauri, and the planets within the habitable zone around that star.

The scientists compiled data on the exoplanet Europa, and it was possible to determine the surface coordinates with great precision, accurate to within a few meters. Theoretically, it would be safe to connect there with the steel protection active in front of the frame. Before establishing the connection, new telescopes that were under development would be delivered to the Space Center to ensure that the measurements would be as precise as possible.

TOWARD EUROPA

When all the components and telescopes had arrived at the hall, the scientists began planning how to position them on Europa's surface. They needed to anchor and calibrate the equipment to explore the region around Proxima Centauri and study the planets within the habitable zone of the star. A relay for radio signals, which would send images and measurements back to Earth, was also to be installed.

Lars started the machine and set the direction, distance, and some coordinates to Europa. All the leading scientists with expertise in planetary research were gathered. When the frame activated and the image flickered on, the monitors only displayed a white screen. No unusual readings were visible. Lars pressed the button to retract the steel plate in front of the frame. There were no visible contours, which made them uncertain if it was snow or ice. Lars guided the machine closer to the surface, and when it seemed like they were near the ground, one of the scientists stepped forward, took a rod, and pressed it against the white surface. The rod only sank a few centimeters before hitting resistance. The scientist scraped back and forth a little, then pulled the rod back to the hall. Now, they could see the tracks in the snow. According to the measurements, there was a small amount of oxygen in the air, but not enough to sustain a human. However, the radiation levels were very low.

Using remote control, they deployed equipment like radar and other measuring instruments, as well as a wheeled drill to take soil samples. They sent out two telescopes: one for visible light and one for infrared light. The telescopes were equipped with tubes to measure sound at different frequencies. A relay for data transmission was also installed on-site. The telescopes were programmed to slowly scan the sky as far as possible. Data would be analyzed later to draw conclusions about their observations.

If the data transmission failed, they would connect via the frame and transfer the data that way. With significant delay, measurement data trickled in from the transmissions from Europa. They occasionally activated the machine to transfer large amounts of data, including images and videos.

There was so much new data that the scientists spent six months analyzing it and developing strategies for the future. During this time, Lars occasionally found himself in Sweden, operating the machines remotely.

CONCLUSIONS FROM EUROPA

After analyzing millions of data points and images, the scientists reached a preliminary conclusion that there were oceans beneath the ice on Europa. In some places, the ice was several kilometers thick, while in other areas, it was only about a hundred meters thick. Oceanographers had previously speculated that there could be liquid water beneath the ice sheet, as the planet's core maintained enough heat to keep the water from freezing. By drilling at spots where the ice was thinner, they were able to investigate the water. It turned out to be saltwater, similar to Earth's oceans. One of the most significant breakthroughs was the discovery of bacteria and traces of life in the water, though no larger life forms had been detected yet. The scientists believed it was possible that larger organisms existed at greater depths where the water was warmer. Above the surface, temperatures were as low as minus 50 degrees, but it might be possible to drill a larger hole to lower a smaller remotely operated robot to conduct further investigations.

Regarding the data from the telescopes, they obtained clear images of the planets orbiting Proxima Centauri. However, they had not yet identified any planets at the perfect distance from the star to be considered habitable. Some planets were outside the habitable zone, and others were too close to the star, resulting in excessively high temperatures. Nevertheless, they continued studying these planets as best they could, given the vast distances involved.

Lars couldn't shake the nagging feeling that there had to be planets in the habitable zone. It seemed illogical to him that none would exist. He thought perhaps the large planets they had observed were blocking smaller ones behind them. This feeling persisted for several weeks, and the scientists tried various methods to search around the large planets for something new.

One morning, when Lars woke up, a series of coordinates and directions suddenly popped into his head. He wrote them down, feeling it was worth investigating. When he arrived at the Space Center, he asked the scientists to point the telescopes at the coordinates he had noted.

As Lars sat in the cafeteria eating lunch, one of the scientists came running toward him, shaking with excitement. In an excited voice, the scientist said, "There's a planet where you wrote down those coordinates! It appears to be twice the size of Earth and lies within the habitable zone, a bit closer to its sun than Earth is to ours. It should have a tropical climate, but we don't know yet if there's any life there. However, it's the only planet we've studied with such a theoretical chance for life. We're continuing to analyze." Lars thanked him for the information and thought, "They, or whatever it is that programmed me, have implanted this knowledge deep inside my mind."

Lars followed the scientist back to the hall and noticed the excitement spreading among the other researchers, who were all talking excitedly over each other. Some came up to congratulate him, asking how he had known this. Lars responded that he had simply guessed there might be something partially obscured by the larger planets.

Based on the discovered data, they continued to carefully measure the distance from Europa to the new planet. They managed to pinpoint a direction and a target, but getting precise coordinates on the planet's surface proved difficult. The suggestion was to connect just outside the planet and take measurements from there.

Lars entered the necessary values and ensured that the steel plate in front of the frame was closed. He activated the monitors and pressed ENTER. On the screen, they saw a blue planet that appeared to have vast oceans. They measured the exact distance to the planet's surface and adjusted the settings to land from space. Lars then shut down the system and prepared for the next step.

The next day, they connected to the coordinates they had calculated the previous day. When the image appeared, they saw a forest in the distance. The measurements indicated there was oxygen at a level slightly higher than Earth's, which wasn't dangerous; in fact, it was advantageous. Gravity was also stronger than Earth's, but not enough to be harmful; it would just make a person feel a bit heavier, and the higher oxygen content would compensate for that. No other dangerous substances were detected. Lars opened the steel plate in front of the frame, and now they could see the landscape even better and more clearly. The temperature gauge showed 30 degrees Celsius in the sun. In front of them stretched a tropical jungle with tall grass and unusually tall trees.

Lars slowly turned the view to the right and saw a plain with scattered trees. As he continued rotating the image about 180 degrees from the original position, they saw large mountains in the distance, with a few snow-covered peaks. The scientists, who had already been excited before contact, were now overwhelmed by what they were witnessing. This was a discovery of historical proportions, possibly the greatest in human history. The implications were staggering, both in terms of possibilities and risks in this new world. Questions flooded their minds: What kind of life might exist there? How far had evolution progressed? They recorded videos of the landscape beyond the frame and decided to shut down and carefully plan their next steps.

A few days later, all the scientists, presidents, and prime ministers from the participating countries gathered at the Space Center. They convened in the conference room, where Collings presented all the discoveries, including those on Europa. But the main news was that they had found a planet that was potentially habitable. The heads of state congratulated them on their success and announced that they would finance whatever was needed for further expeditions.

Collings announced that each participating country would be allowed to select scientists to bring to the new world, along with a number of military personnel who would act as peacekeepers to protect the researchers. He emphasized that this was not about going in to shoot anyone or anything since they couldn't yet be sure who or what dominated the world. Even an ant could turn out to be the highest intelligence on this planet. He stressed the importance of approaching cautiously and suggested they establish a base camp near the spot where they had first connected. The proposal was to use peaceful drones to explore the nearby area and gather more data.

He concluded by announcing that the scientists would have a meeting the next day to plan how to proceed.

BASE CAMP

The planning was complete, and they were ready to transport materials to the planet. They had prepared everything they might need. Lars connected the machine, set the directions and coordinates, and pressed ENTER. In the window, they saw the location where they had last been. Small electric loaders moved out crates, tools, and various measuring instruments. They also brought containers that had been converted into different laboratories. To ensure a steady power supply, they set up several solar panels to power all the equipment and charge the electric vehicles. Outside the base camp, they installed sensors that could alert them if anything or anyone approached.

They noted that this planet rotated more slowly around its sun. A day here lasted 27 hours, as the planet was twice the size of Earth. The base camp was enclosed with strong fences, and they installed a gate that could open and close when they needed to leave the area for reconnaissance missions.

In the distance, they could hear bird sounds and see something moving in the air. The biologists prepared for their soil tests and began examining the trees a bit further away. The vegetation around the trees was dense, limiting visibility. They knew they needed to be cautious as there could be unknown dangers. Soldiers took positions overlooking both the trees and the plains next to the base camp. It was decided that researchers would always be accompanied by at least two soldiers when working outside the camp.

One team was tasked with using small drones to map the area around the base camp. Their first priority was to survey the nearby area, but the plan was to gradually explore farther out.

Step by step, they would create maps of the region for future expeditions.

Inside one of the containers, they had installed a frame with an accompanying machine. This one was simplified, requiring only a power switch to automatically calibrate the direction and coordinates back to the center of the hall on Earth. Everyone at the camp had a communication device to send and receive messages. Every other day, they would open a communication link to transfer data, videos, and other information to the researchers who remained on Earth. After the research leader, Collings, verified that everything was set up and functioning as planned, he gave the green light for them to begin exploring this new world.

EXPLORATION OF THE PLANET

The biologists were the first to head out to collect samples of the soil and plants. They moved toward the forest's edge and gathered samples from the trees, including bark, leaves, and needle-like leaves that were almost half a meter long. On the ground, they discovered tracks resembling both hooves and paws, which puzzled them. They photographed the tracks for later analysis. When they returned to the base camp, they felt unusually tired, an effect of the higher gravity that made their bodies feel heavier.

The drone teams deployed their units according to a predetermined pattern. When they flew over the forest, they could only see the ground in a few spots. At one point, they startled a large bird with a wingspan of over a meter and a heavy body. On Earth, such a bird would likely have had difficulty flying with such a large body, but the higher oxygen levels here made it possible.

The drones flying over the steppe discovered some large animals grazing in the grass. They were gray, with two long horns, long legs, and heavy bodies. Even these creatures seemed oversized compared to what would be possible on Earth. The zoologists would study these videos closely later.

A third drone flew toward the mountains visible on the horizon. Below the drone stretched deep ravines, and in some of them, rivers flowed abundantly. Here, they spotted various large animals resembling dinosaurs, but with some differences. They captured footage of a large, agile predator attacking another creature, but the predator lost after receiving a powerful kick that sent it flying. The predator had long, sharp teeth and fur in all the colors of the rainbow.

When the drones returned to the base camp to be recharged, images, videos, and coordinates were transmitted to begin mapping the area. Several researchers analyzed the footage and concluded that the animals on this planet were much larger than their Earth counterparts, with some creatures even larger than elephants. The abundant food supply was likely a contributing factor to their size. This resembled Earth's history during the time when dinosaurs roamed the planet. The scientists speculated that this planet was in a similar evolutionary phase as Earth during the Cretaceous period, but it was not as old as Earth.

Given their discoveries, the scientists realized that this world could be dangerous for humans. They recommended increased vigilance and reinforcements of the fence around the base camp, possibly with electrified barriers for added security. They also installed powerful spotlights to illuminate the area if they heard anything suspicious outside the camp.

The biologists reached a similar conclusion: the plants here were much larger and stronger. The difference from Earth during the Cretaceous period was that there were both coniferous and deciduous trees. On Earth during the same period, giant ferns were the primary food source for animals. It wasn't surprising that everything was larger here, with constant tropical temperatures and abundant rainfall, which they deduced from the many rivers. They realized they needed to be prepared for rain and humidity, as they didn't know if the area experienced monsoon rains. It was important not to stay away from the camp for too long and always to have guards with them who could defend them if necessary. The guards were instructed to first try using tranquilizers if they encountered anything dangerous. Their automatic rifles were equipped with dual barrels for this purpose.

Everyone had received specially designed watches that were calibrated to the planet's 27-hour day. They waited to see when the sun would set and when it would rise again. The sun stayed at its zenith for many more hours than on Earth, and at 11:00 PM local time, it began to slowly dip behind the horizon, creating a spectacular red sky.

After most of the team had gone to bed for the night, except for a few guards, they were suddenly awakened by loud noises near the camp. Since it was dark, they couldn't see what was causing the noise. When they turned on a spotlight, they saw a few large animals standing and staring toward the camp. When the light was directed at them, the animals panicked and fled out of sight. It seemed the animals were afraid of the bright light. No one had gotten a clear look at the animals due to the distance, so they decided to set up night cameras for the following night. Once the spotlights were turned off, no further sounds were heard nearby, but a faint howling could be heard far off.

At 8:00 AM local time, the sun rose again, meaning it was light for 18 hours a day. In the morning, when they examined the area outside the base camp, they couldn't find any tracks from the animals they had seen during the night. The zoologists speculated that these creatures might not be particularly fast, but they could likely jump high and far, given their hooves at the front and paw-like back legs. They wondered if the fence was high enough to keep the animals out and speculated that these creatures might be nocturnal since they seemed to shy away from bright light.

After studying the maps created by the drones, they determined that it would be possible to travel along the forest's edge in vehicles, avoiding the deep ravines. All vehicles were equipped with solar panels, meaning they could essentially travel indefinitely as long as the weather was clear. The vehicles were designed for off-road travel and reinforced to withstand external pressures. They were also equipped with cameras to monitor the surroundings and had communication systems to keep in contact with other vehicles and the base camp, as long as they weren't too far away. The vehicles could carry several people and were equipped to allow rest if it became late and they couldn't return to the base camp before nightfall. The plan was for three cars to participate in the first exploration journey, with one car filled with guards and the other two carrying three scientists each.

The First Expedition

Around ten o'clock, three vehicles set off along the route they had planned, based on the maps they had carefully studied. Their position was continuously monitored to ensure a quick response in case anything happened. They had also contacted Lars on Earth to have an emergency signal ready if a serious situation arose. Each time the machines connected, the coordinates were automatically updated to mark the vehicles' latest position. They had also transported a helicopter to the planet, which would only be used in emergencies, as the engine noise could easily reveal their location. The use of the helicopter could only be authorized by Collings.

The vehicles moved quickly and covered several miles in a short time. The terrain was easy to drive on, and the roads were clear. Far off on the horizon, they could see a column of smoke rising into the sky. Their interest was immediately piqued, and they wondered what was causing the smoke. Suddenly, through the cameras, they saw a large and powerful animal running at high speed straight toward them. Before they could react, the animal crashed violently into the second vehicle, which overturned and slid a short distance on the ground. The guards in the first vehicle quickly opened a hatch and aimed at the animal, ready to shoot if it turned toward them.

The animal stopped by the overturned vehicle, snorting and raising its head to sniff the air, as if trying to identify the scents around it. It stood still for a long time, surveying the area. It was clear that the animal was aware of the other two vehicles, which remained motionless. The animal swayed back and forth, unsure of what to do next. A call came over the radio from the first vehicle, asking how the occupants of the rammed vehicle were doing. They responded that everyone was fine, just a bit shaken.

"Everyone, stay still and don't reveal yourselves," said the guard in the first vehicle, his voice calm but firm.

After a while, the animal turned around and slowly walked back toward the forest. They waited a few more minutes before one of the guards, who had been keeping watch on the forest, signaled that it was safe. The others quickly moved to the overturned vehicle to help their colleagues out. Using a winch attached to the second vehicle, they pulled the overturned car back up so that all four wheels were once again firmly on the ground. After a quick inspection, they determined that the vehicle hadn't sustained any serious damage, just a few minor dents where the animal had struck.

This time, they had been lucky. They now realized they had been too confident during the drive and had lost focus. They needed to be more cautious going forward and always be prepared for the unexpected.

After taking a short break for lunch, they sent up a drone to survey the terrain ahead, in the direction of the smoke. The terrain appeared to be similar to what they had already driven through, with no major obstacles in sight. They decided to be extra vigilant and carefully observe their surroundings as they continued.

After lunch, they resumed their journey, but this time only made short stops if they thought they saw something move. They soon realized it was just the wind or small animals moving in the vegetation. This time, everyone had buckled their seatbelts tightly, ready for something similar to happen again.

The Discovery at the Smoke

They approached the location where the smoke was visible. A small hill lay ahead, and they stopped the vehicles to cautiously sneak up the slope. Upon reaching the top, they took out their binoculars and focused them on the smoke. Down below, near the fire, they saw creatures resembling apes, jumping and leaping around the flames. They appeared to be a primitive race, possibly in an early stage of evolution, similar to ancestors of early humans. What puzzled them was that these creatures had a fire going. The scientists, who had also climbed the hill, noted that the creatures had a hollowed-out stone functioning as a simple hearth. This led them to suspect that, like the earliest humans on Earth, these beings might have utilized a fire caused by a lightning strike rather than knowing how to start one themselves.

The scientists decided not to make contact with the creatures. By observing their movements and gestures, they could see that the beings didn't seem capable of communication through speech. Instead, they used body language and gestured animatedly but without any form of spoken language. It was best not to disturb them.

The group made a detour around the creatures' camp and continued their exploration. According to the local clock, the sun would soon set, so they decided to camp for the night. They parked the vehicles in a triangle, close to each other, so they could gather in the middle to discuss the day's observations. It was fascinating to see a species that might be in the early stages of human development, but it was too early to draw any conclusions. They had plenty of supplies and decided to continue their exploration before returning to base camp.

During the night, the vehicles' radar detected movement nearby. They put on their night vision goggles and could now see the animals more clearly. They were twice the size of wolves and moved quickly and gracefully. Suddenly, they saw one of them leap over some other animals, reaching an estimated height of three meters in the air. The guard in the driver's cabin ordered the others to turn on the floodlights before the animals got too close. All three vehicles switched on their powerful lights simultaneously. The animals stopped abruptly and let out cries of pain before quickly fleeing back into the forest. It seemed the bright lights caused them great discomfort, and they quickly retreated. The crew in the vehicles could relax again and return to sleep.

The next morning, they inspected the ground where the animals had been, and the tracks they found were the same as those seen outside the base camp. After breakfast, eaten in the safety of the vehicles, the guards sent drones in various directions to survey the terrain and determine if it was possible to continue the journey.

One of the guards piloting a drone shouted out; he had seen something. Everyone gathered around the monitor and saw two parallel tracks resembling a simple forest path, possibly created by carts. The tracks stretched straight ahead, about five kilometers away. It still looked like they could drive there without much difficulty, and the vehicles' batteries were almost fully charged.

After packing up from breakfast, they resumed their journey toward the forest path. After about twenty minutes, they arrived. Upon closer inspection, it was clear that the tracks were wheel ruts. They looked around and saw that the forest lay on one side while the wheel tracks continued out of the trees and down into a valley. Here, the grass was tall, green, and lush. Further down in the valley, they could see large animals grazing on the grass.

They decided to drive down into the valley. Dark clouds began to gather in the sky and were moving toward them quickly. Soon, a violent rainstorm broke out, and visibility became nearly nonexistent. They were ordered to stop and wait out the rain, which pounded hard on the vehicles' roofs. After a while, the rain was followed by powerful lightning and thunderclaps. It was a serious thunderstorm, but the lightning stayed distant, and it seemed the storm wouldn't come any closer.

The rain and thunder continued for several hours before it finally subsided. Small streams formed along the road down the valley as water flowed rapidly. When the clouds finally cleared and the sun emerged, the ground quickly began to warm up, and mist and steam rose into the air. After a while, the ground began to dry up, and they tried slowly driving one of the vehicles to see if the road had become too muddy. Fortunately, the road was as solid as it had been before the storm. They realized that with such heavy rainfall, it was no wonder the vegetation was so lush. They had previously wondered how the plant life could be so green and vibrant despite the intense tropical heat, but now they had their answer.

The Valley

As they approached the bottom of the valley, they saw a large river flowing through it. It was still possible to drive alongside the river. After traveling a bit upstream, they saw more similar roads joining the one they were on, and the path became twice as wide. It was now important to proceed cautiously and use the drones to inspect the road ahead. They could drive half a mile at a time without any issues. The next time they stopped and deployed the drones, they spotted buildings that resembled houses. They stopped at a vantage point and studied the houses and their surroundings. They could see no movement in the area for several hours. They agreed to rotate guard duties to keep watch. Evening came, and they still hadn't seen any signs of life. Once again, they parked the vehicles in a triangle.

They reported back to base camp, which they managed to do by climbing a nearby hill. They relayed what they had seen and provided their coordinates. They were instructed to stay put, and the base camp would be relocated to their location. They were to break down the camp and, with Lars' help, connect the machine to bring in most of the equipment, except for various measurement devices and the fence. Once this was completed, they would connect to the location where the three vehicles were stationed, a bit off the road they had come from and not visible from the area with the houses below.

It took a couple of days to load everything into the hall at Space Center, and Lars set the new coordinates for the site and started the machine. Once the connection was established, everything was unloaded, and they organized a new base camp.

While setting up the new base camp, scouts were sent out to investigate the houses up close. As they approached the houses, they still saw no signs of movement. They crept up to the house walls and listened for any sounds. Hearing nothing, they cautiously approached the door. The door was ajar and appeared to be broken. They peered inside and saw a table and a chair, but otherwise, the house was empty. The floor was covered in dirt and old leaves. They went to another house and found it in the same condition: completely empty and dirty. They examined house after house, and all were abandoned. They returned and reported that the area was completely deserted.

A new investigation team with different guards was sent out. They launched drones to explore the surrounding area and discovered more houses that appeared abandoned. Further away, they saw more solidly built two-story houses. However, they saw no signs of life nearby. The drone flew closer to the houses and pointed the camera at the windows, where it also appeared deserted. They could see footprints on the yard leading away along the road. Analysis of the footage showed that all the houses were abandoned. Something must have happened that caused everyone to leave long ago.

It was decided that three vehicles would follow the road and try to find a house that seemed inhabited. They set off and were able to maintain a high speed on the wide road. At one point, they saw an animal grazing on the meadows next to the river from a distance. They drove for a long time without seeing anything. After traveling two hundred miles, they stopped for a break while the guards maneuvered the drones forward along the road and far to the sides. They saw some cottages that seemed abandoned. After the break, they continued for another hundred miles without seeing anything. Soon it began to get dark, and they looked for a spot where they could have a good view of the surrounding area. They had been searching for roads connecting to the one they were on but had found none, only the single road. They managed to contact the base camp and report their findings. As before, Collings would confer with the others. Once again, the decision was made to move the base camp to the location where the vehicles had stopped. They would soon consider using the helicopter for reconnaissance, but they preferred not to do so yet.

During the night, they were once again awakened by a distant sound. When they exited the vehicles, they could hear that the sound was coming from afar. After a while, they saw a light far away reflected against the sky. After an hour or so, the light disappeared, and it was quiet again. They went back to sleep and planned to investigate the area in the morning.

After breakfast, they set off and calculated where the light might have come from during the night. As they approached the place they thought the light came from, they stopped and began to inspect the area with the drones. One drone flew over a grove of tall trees and discovered a massive building with high fences all around, but no other activity was visible. They flew slowly high above the building and examined the area. The fence had a large gate that was open. They recorded the coordinates for the building and contacted base camp. They requested Lars to connect to the inside of the building to see if anyone or anything was there. Base camp contacted Lars on Earth and explained what they wanted. Lars connected to the coordinates and saw through his window that the inside of the building was empty, except for a few small rooms. He informed base camp that it was empty. When the team in the vehicles received the message, they drove to the building and parked outside. The guards crept along the side of the building up to a large door. On the door was a sign with symbols they did not understand. They carefully opened the door and shone a light inside to check for any dangerous devices or traps. Finding nothing, they entered the building. Inside, there was a table with some kind of device and texts on a paper beside it. None of the text was comprehensible, and the device was completely unfamiliar. They called the scientists to examine the paper and the device without touching anything.

After a while, a linguist from Earth joined via the connection Lars had set up. They took pictures of the text and transmitted them to Earth for analysis. No one could decipher the symbols. However, the linguist there said that the symbols resembled something he had seen before, though he could not quite remember what. He also examined the symbols on the door. They searched the building and found more signs with the same kind of symbols.

On Earth, there was intense work to try to decipher the symbols. There was no doubt that it was a language. By coincidence, Lars noticed the text and was surprised. He understood most of the symbols. It was a description of how to communicate with the device.

"Damn, have they also installed a language in my head?" Lars said to himself.

He thought this might be proof that he had come to the right planet, the one intended for him. Lars translated the text and informed the linguist in the large building. The linguist began to figure out what the symbols looked like and what they meant.

He managed to decipher the other signs, or at least he thought he did. On the door, it read: "Keep the door closed."

The scientists were instructed not to attempt to start the machine, only to try to understand how it worked based on the instructions.

The emptiness of the building was mysterious. They had seen a light coming from it. Could it be that they had evacuated the house just yesterday and they missed it? Or did they know they were nearby and became frightened? But it didn't seem logical for them to light a strong light if they were afraid of being discovered.

They sent out the drones again to explore the road ahead. The drones flew nearly ten miles without seeing any vehicles or transports. A team of three vehicles continued along the road. After driving a hundred miles, the landscape changed; it went up and down in steep inclines. However, there were no problems for the vehicles since their batteries typically lasted for eighty miles. After traveling another fifty miles and reaching a height, they spotted what looked like a city with tall buildings. The buildings appeared somewhat futuristic with spires on top. They decided to stay where they were to get a better overview of the city. They estimated the distance between the city's outskirts to be five to six kilometers. While studying the city, they saw an object flying in and landing in the middle of the city. They measured their own coordinates and noted the coordinates of the location where the object landed. They tried to contact the latest base camp but were unsuccessful; the distance was too great, and the terrain they had traveled through caused poor coverage. One of the vehicles drove back until they could reestablish contact with the base camp.

For the third time, the base camp was moved, this time to a location a bit away from the city. As they scouted over the city, they saw some figures on the edge of the built-up area. Upon closer inspection with zoom, they saw that these were beings walking on two legs, very tall and slender. They could not see any weapons in the beings' hands. Collings, together with the guards and scientists, planned the next steps. The question was whether they should dare to reveal themselves and approach the city. Meanwhile, they unloaded equipment, including Lars' small machine that enabled contact with Earth. The tactic was to avoid doing anything that could be perceived as a confrontation. They waited and continued to study the city. For several days, they observed flying objects landing in the city center, but no objects leaving the city.

The City

One day, one of the beings suddenly appeared on the road near them. No one had seen it approach. At first, it stood and looked at them, and it seemed like it extended its arms to show it was unarmed, or at least that's how they interpreted it. Collings stepped forward on the road, took a few steps, and also extended his arms to show he was unarmed. Collings slowly walked towards the being, and it did the same. When they were a couple of meters apart, they stopped. Up close, the being looked human but had a body that was slim and one and a half times the length of an average human. It appeared male. The man placed his hand over his chest as a greeting, and Collings did the same. The man said something unintelligible, and Collings responded that he did not understand. The man reached into a pocket of the long brown leather coat he was wearing, and Collings recoiled in fear. But the man pulled out a piece of paper and handed it to Collings. He looked at the note and saw that it only contained one word: "LARS". Collings looked up at the man, nodded, and gestured in a sweeping motion towards the sky and beyond.

The man nodded and turned back. He walked slowly down the road and disappeared over a small rise. They waited for him to appear at the next rise, but he did not come. They waited for a long time before someone went up to the rise and looked. There was no one there. They found it strange, as they could see to the sides and did not see anyone walking there either. When Collings returned, he showed the note to the others.

Collings said, "It must mean that they want to meet him; I can't interpret it any other way. Lars seemed to understand their language."

The mood in the camp calmed a bit after the encounter. It did not seem as though the beings were hostile, and they had shown that they knew humans were here. They contacted Earth and reported the encounter with the native man and showed the note they had received. They would talk to Lars and ask if he would be willing to go there. After a moment of consideration, he agreed. He just needed to make some preparations.

He programmed the computer so that it could only connect to the current base camp. He created a simplified control panel with one button to start the machine and another to turn it off.

He informed one of the technicians that he must not touch the computer and could only press the buttons. He also instructed the technician to turn off the machine once he had passed through the window and not to restart it until he received instructions from the base camp.

Lars started the machine by pressing the button, went up the gangway, and stepped through the window. When he appeared at the base camp, Collings was there to welcome him. He showed Lars around the camp and pointed out where he had met the stranger from the city. Lars understood that the stranger had used a machine to get there from the city. "I'll go down to the city myself; no one is to come with me!" said Lars.

Glob

He began walking down the road. It was quite a distance, and he did so deliberately slowly so that they would see he was alone and posed no threat. As he approached the edge of the city, one of the beings was waiting for him. The being looked exactly as they had described: dressed in leather and a long coat.

He walked up to Lars and extended his hand. Lars greeted him and noticed that the man's hand was soft with long fingers and slightly cooler skin. The man began to speak, and Lars was surprised to find that he understood what was being said.

The man said, "Welcome here; you have completed the task we asked of you. We apologize for using you in this way. We have long studied your kind without revealing ourselves, and you were genetically suited for the possibility of implanting knowledge into your consciousness. I hope this has not caused you any problems."

"No, it's no trouble," Lars replied in their language. "It has been a very interesting journey for me. As you probably knew, my interest in space and the dream of meeting other life forms was a lifelong ambition. I am grateful for this opportunity."

"My name is Kurel, and I am a member of our planet's council. Would you mind coming inside to speak with me and the council?" Kurel asked.

"That's fine," Lars replied.

Kurel led the way and opened a door through which they walked. On the other side, there were beautiful statuettes and flower arrangements along the walls. In the center was a conveyor belt that began to move as they stepped onto it. It moved fairly quickly but still felt secure.

They were presumably being taken to the city center. When they reached the end of the conveyor belt, there were several other belts extending in different directions. From the center, there were several doors between the belts, and they opened one of the doors and asked Lars to follow them inside. Inside, there was a corridor with a low wall full of various trees and flowers. The ceiling allowed sunlight to illuminate the corridor. At regular intervals, there were openings leading to house-like structures.

After passing a few openings, they reached a larger driveway that led to a gold-glittering building. They walked up the driveway and entered the building. Many people, similar to Kurel in build, were sitting behind desks and at round tables, drinking some kind of beverage. As they went further in, they came to a room with many seats around a large oval table. About ten people were scattered around the table, but the head end was empty. Kurel asked Lars to sit next to him at the head end. They sat down, and someone came forward and placed a glass and a pitcher of water on the table.

Kurel began to speak: "We welcome Lars, who represents the planet Earth today. He has been pleased with the task we gave him. He also managed to manufacture the machine that we helped him understand and used it in a good and democratic manner, without revealing how the machine was built."

Kurel turned to Lars and said, "We really appreciate you doing everything to come here. Even though we look different, our races are very similar in terms of our genetics. Our planet, like yours, has developed over billions of years. We may not have advanced as far in all respects; you and we have developed differently, but we are equally valuable. We are glad that when you came here, you respected our animals and our nature. Our world has been a peaceful, democratic, and technocratic society for several thousand years. We do not and cannot inflict violence on any other beings. This is something we know you appreciate, as we followed you on Earth before we chose you as our representative to your world. However, we have had a problem for many years that has caused us great sorrow. There are other races on other planets that do not share our morals. They have attacked us and killed more than half of our population. In short, they are trying to exterminate us. What has prevented us from being completely wiped out is our knowledge of the machine, which you now also know about. But as a race, we cannot retaliate; it is not in our nature to cause harm, and therefore we cannot defend ourselves either. That is why we wanted you to come here and see how we are treated and killed by these beings from a planet not more than a light-year away. Of course, it is up to you whether you wish to help us! When we studied your Earth, we saw that you have an overpopulated planet that you are in the process of destroying."

Kurel continued: "What we can offer you is that, if the leaders of your planet agree, humans would have the opportunity to voluntarily move here to our planet. As you have seen, we have lush vegetation and both vegetables and, for those who wish, game to hunt. But this is on the condition that you do not start factories with emissions that harm the planet. We offer areas that are larger than your Earth, where you can independently make decisions about your path. We hope, however, that we can co-govern for the benefit of all. We know that you have leaders who may not be very democratic, and that is largely due to increasing congestion and selfishness. We believe and hope that we could achieve such a reality together. You have the ability and technology to counter the enemy we face."

In conclusion, Kurel said: "We do not expect an answer from you now; you must present our wishes to your leaders. However, we expect that you do not reveal the technology for building the machine. As you know, it can be used for harmful purposes."

Lars stood up, looked out over the assembly, and said: "Thank you for giving me this knowledge. I will preserve it well. I will gladly present your request and hope that we can reach an agreement. I truly understand your situation, and I am genuinely upset by injustices wherever they occur. There is room for everyone. I am sure there are many habitable planets in space."

As he concluded his speech, the attendees applauded loudly. Lars and Kurel shook hands and thanked each other. Lars announced that he would immediately speak with the leaders. Kurel accompanied Lars back to the conveyor belt, and they went back to the outer door. There, Kurel informed Lars that they could contact each other via a transmitter he gave him. He also handed over four earpieces, which Kurel explained would translate from Earth's language to their planet's language. "We call this planet Glob," said Kurel. "Until we meet again, goodbye!"

Lars opened the door and walked slowly back to the camp.

Back at the camp, they had become anxious since he had been gone for so long; they feared he might have been captured. When they saw him coming out, they breathed a sigh of relief.

They asked in unison how it was down there and if he understood what was said. He silenced them with his hand and said he would tell them if they stopped asking so many questions.

He first described what it looked like inside, how beautiful it was with the flowers, trees, and buildings. Then he provided an explanation by recounting their history and what they had endured from the attacking beings. He mentioned that they needed help to stop them

THE PEACEKEEPING FORCE

The decision to try to help was an easy one. They had received the green light from the world leaders. They would gather a couple of battalions of the most skilled soldiers from every country. It would take a few weeks to organize and equip such a group.

They asked Lars for more information about the nature of the attacks and what kind of weapons the attackers had. They wanted to know how the attackers were being transported to this planet. Above all, they wondered where the attackers' planet was located and how far it was from the world he was currently on.

Lars went into the city to talk with Kurel. He learned that the attackers arrived in spaceships that positioned themselves in orbit around Glob. They had smaller spacecraft that they flew down into the atmosphere and landed with. They had bombs and rockets of a model similar to Earth's weapons. They came at regular intervals and primarily targeted infrastructure. Because this had been going on for many years, many of the inhabitants had been killed. The attackers knew they faced little resistance. But the people of Glob didn't understand why their world was being attacked. Previously, they had had some form of contact with one another and had met long enough to learn each other's language. They had sent several messages to the attackers, asking why they were being assaulted, but the only response they received was: "Because you deserve it." No other explanations. This led them to perceive the attackers as extremely evil.

Lars asked how the people of Glob traveled, apart from using the machine, of course. They had flying vehicles of various sizes. They could also travel in space using these crafts. They had radar systems that alerted them when the attackers positioned themselves outside the planet. But they had never made any weapons to use against them. If they were to receive help, they could provide the military with a number of crafts of different sizes.

Kurel explained that, of course, they had started to build shelters and reinforce public buildings. They had constructed force fields that could withstand missile hits, but it wasn't possible to protect everyone. In recent years, the attackers had never destroyed uninhabited areas, so the animals had fared well, despite everything.

Lars relayed all this information to the defense force and leadership on Earth. For someone from Earth, it was strange that they didn't defend themselves, given their vast technical knowledge. But according to Kurel, they had not practiced any violence for many years and were true pacifists.

It was decided to gather two battalions from all the countries participating in the project. In the base camp, they planned the reception and devised a strategy based on the information they had received about where the attacks had occurred most frequently. They had obtained local maps covering most of the planet. There were areas that were uninhabited, partly due to inaccessibility and because there hadn't been a need for settlements, as there weren't that many inhabitants on Glob. It's important to remember that this planet is twice the size of Earth. In terms of climate, there are polar regions with ice and snow, large seas, and lakes spread across the planet. There are areas with underdeveloped animals that have evolved into humanoid, prehistoric creatures, including the ape-like people they saw around the fire. There were also regions they hadn't explored in jungles with dense trees in the warmest areas. There were signs that indigenous people might inhabit these areas.

DEPLOYMENT OF TROOPS

Lars had prepared to program the machine to designate locations where soldiers could be deployed across various areas of the planet. As time passed, soldiers, civilian technicians, and supplies were sent to different camps. A system for monitoring space was organized. They had prepared for the possibility that the attackers would come from the neighboring planet, as they had previously, so they could raise an alert if they saw anything unusual. Additionally, they equipped the flying crafts they had been given with cannons and projectiles.

They had not seen the neighboring planet before, as it had been directly behind Glob, obscured from view. That planet was slightly smaller than Glob but larger than Earth. They did not know if or when an attack might occur, so they carefully monitored any movements in space toward the other planet.

One day, they received a warning that there appeared to be activity in space. The peacekeeping force was placed on high alert. They tracked the movements and saw a large ship enter orbit around Glob. After a while, when the ship passed over inhabited areas, many smaller spacecraft emerged from the large vessel and descended through the atmosphere. The force waited, as they had orders not to strike first. They were only to respond if they were attacked and bombed.

When the crafts were in the air above the inhabited cities, they began firing at buildings. The soldiers were then given the go-ahead to return fire! As artillery began firing at the crafts, it became clear that the attackers were caught off guard, flying disorganized in all directions. The military managed to shoot down one of the crafts and saw two individuals parachuting out.

The soldiers immediately regrouped and moved toward the area where the parachutes were expected to land. They spotted the two parachutes approaching the ground. When the individuals landed, they were quickly surrounded by the soldiers. Using hand signals, the soldiers indicated that they should get down on the ground. The individuals looked very much like humans but with slightly larger-than-normal heads. They lay down on the ground and raised their arms in a gesture of surrender. The soldiers handcuffed them and took them to their camp. The remaining attacking crafts returned to the large mothership and quickly fled.

The prisoners were transported to the main camp, where attempts were made to interrogate them, but they didn't understand the questions and spoke a completely different language than the inhabitants of Glob. Upon searching the individuals, it was discovered that they were not both men—one was a man, and the other was a woman! Both tried to speak their language and gestured. They pointed to the sky, then to the ground, and lifted their hands to illustrate a large explosion. Collings, who was attempting to interrogate them, was puzzled by their gestures and wondered why they were indicating a bomb falling and exploding on the ground. Collings was wearing the translator they had received from Kurel, but it wasn't translating anything. He contacted Lars and asked him to request Kurel to program a translator, as Kurel had mentioned they had learned the attackers' language.

Lars went to the city and told the guard that he wanted to meet Kurel. Since the guard recognized him, he let him in and pointed to which conveyor belt he should take. When he arrived, he walked to the door he had previously entered and strolled past the beautiful corridors toward the council's house. He knocked on the door and was let into the hall. Kurel welcomed him and appeared happy.

"You managed to scare them off before anything serious happened," Kurel said.

"Yes, as soon as we started firing, they got confused since they had never encountered any resistance before. We've captured a couple of prisoners and want to interrogate them, but we don't understand what they're saying. You mentioned you had learned their language. We're wondering if you could program a translator for us?" Lars asked.

"But we can interrogate them ourselves!" Kurel replied.

"No," Lars said. "Since we've been tasked with protecting you, we also want to conduct the interrogation."

"Okay, we'll try to program one, but it will take a day or so before you can have it," Kurel said.

After two days, a guard from the city arrived and delivered the earpieces to them. He explained that the prisoners would receive a translation if they wore the earpieces. They thanked the guard, who turned and headed back to the city.

THE INTERROGATIONS

They brought the male prisoner into a room and chained him to a chair. Collings and Lars led the interrogation. They began by introducing themselves and explaining that they were a peacekeeping force from another planet, tasked with protecting Glob from attacks.

"Why are you attacking Glob?" Collings asked.

The man responded, "We are forced to avenge their actions."

"Why do you need to avenge them?" Collings asked.

"They've been bombing us for years and killing many of our people. We have to defend ourselves," the man said.

"We've spoken with the council here on Glob, and they say they haven't done anything to you. They don't practice violence," Collings replied.

"But it's true that they've been bombing us for years, even though we've never seen how they arrive or how they do it," the man said.

"What do you mean you haven't seen them?" Collings asked.

"Suddenly, bombs are inside our city halls, and we don't know how they got there since we're constantly monitoring. All of a sudden, a bomb explodes, and we can't see on our cameras where it came from. They just appear out of nowhere and explode," the man explained.

Lars pulled Collings aside and asked him to turn off the translator. Lars shared his suspicion:

"According to Kurel, only they have the ability to build a machine like the one I constructed. He told me I'm the only outsider with that knowledge. But everything the man says suggests that someone with that technology is doing this to them."

"Could it be someone from here using the technology? And why? Is Kurel telling us the truth?" Collings pondered.

After the interrogation with the man, they took him out and brought in the woman. They asked her the same questions and received the same answers.

The woman said, "All the children they've killed! My own daughter was injured and is in the hospital with serious injuries," she said, breaking into tears. "Those damn murderers."

They asked her when the most recent attack against them was, and she said it was a week ago, which was why they launched their assault now. They ordered the soldiers to lock up the prisoners but to treat them well and provide them with food.

"What do we do now?" Collings asked.

"I don't think we should say anything to Kurel at this stage. Somehow, we need to think this through. Is Kurel telling the truth, and if so, who is committing these acts? Is there someone here on Glob who stands to gain by provoking the neighboring planet? Could someone have another agenda?" Lars replied.

They agreed that Lars would speak to Kurel and try to gather information without revealing his suspicions. He would say that the prisoners refused to speak. During his next visit to the city, Lars met Kurel and told him that they had not been able to get the prisoners to talk, but they would continue the interrogations.

As they continued talking, a discussion arose, creating an opportunity for Lars to casually ask if the technology he had been given could track when connections were made. Kurel replied that they had developed a system to detect if a connection had been made. Their own machines had a logging system to prevent misuse. Only a few were trained to use it, and the technology was only employed for research purposes and with caution, as it could be misused.

Lars asked if they had experienced any problems with it. Kurel said that a few years ago, some council members had suggested conquering other planets to strengthen their own, but the idea had not gained support. Lars asked if he could see their logs to check all the connections they had made since arriving on Glob. Kurel said it would be a pleasure to show him how the system worked.

They went to a terminal, and Kurel pulled up all the connections they had logged since their arrival. Lars reviewed the list and noticed that there had been a connection a week ago. He cautiously asked what that connection was. Kurel pressed the timestamp and looked a bit puzzled.

"But what's this?" he muttered to himself. He searched further and said, "Strange, it says we had a connection on that day, but that can't be right. It's coming from here, and we didn't have any projects in progress. I see it's from a small terminal in our research department. I'm supposed to authorize all connections, and I haven't received any requests."

Lars thought for a moment and decided to reveal his suspicion, as it was clear something was wrong.

"That's why I've been so inquisitive. I suspected that someone here has another agenda and is actually attacking the other world."

He explained what the prisoners had said and how it seemed that someone had connected a machine and planted bombs on their planet. Kurel went pale and was about to rush off, but Lars stopped him, suggesting they investigate quietly and catch the culprit in the act. "Could it be one of those who wanted to take over other planets?" he asked.

Kurel calmed down and agreed with Lars that they needed to check this secretly and tell no one else.

He checked the dates and times of the connections and confirmed that there had been multiple connections a week before the recent attack.

"I have a few relatives I trust who can install a hidden camera. I'll ask them to program it so that the next time someone tries to connect, they'll get an error message saying a relay isn't working, and I'll receive an alert. That way, I'll have some time to catch them in the act when they try to locate the faulty relay," Kurel said.

"I hope you'll notify me when it happens," Lars said.

"Of course I will," Kurel replied.

Lars returned to the base camp and informed Collings of what they had discovered. He told him that Kurel had been genuinely surprised when he found out about the connection to the other planet.

THE CONSPIRACY

Four days later, Lars received a message asking him to come to the city. When he arrived, Kurel informed him that everything had gone exactly as planned. They had both filmed those attempting to connect to the other planet and received an alert that allowed Kurel to gather a guard unit. They went to the research department and caught the culprits red-handed. They had loaded several bombs by the window, intending to throw them out during the connection.

Kurel explained that this had happened two days ago. The previous day, they had interrogated those present in the room, and sure enough, two of them were council members who wanted to take over other planets. Some of the others had minor roles in the acts; a couple of technicians believed the whole operation was sanctioned by the leadership. They also named another council member who was apparently the ringleader.

"We now have documented evidence and have allowed our court to issue sentences for national treason," Kurel said. "The verdict comes tomorrow! You're welcome to attend if you'd like."

"Thank you, I'd be interested in observing your justice system," Lars replied.

The next day, Lars sat in the courtroom, listening to the charges and the evidence presented. The accused denied the crimes, except for a couple of technicians who admitted their involvement, thinking it was authorized by the leadership. The judge summarized the charges and then instructed the jury to deliberate. There was a recess, and people began talking to one another, occasionally glancing at Lars, whom most had never seen before. In their eyes, he was an outsider, an alien!

After half an hour, the jury returned, and everyone took their seats. The jury handed a piece of paper to the judge, who read the verdict aloud: Three council members were found guilty of high treason, the most serious crime one could commit. Three of the technicians received warnings, and another was sentenced to community service.

The judge declared that the guilty council members would be "erased."

Lars was taken aback and thought, *Do they have the death penalty? Kurel said they were pacifists.*

Afterward, Lars asked Kurel how the executions would be carried out.

"Executions? No, no, we absolutely don't do that," Kurel replied.

"But the judge said they would be erased," Lars said.

"Ah, you misunderstood! No, they will be reprogrammed with our technology. We can alter their brains so that they become regular workers, and they won't remember having been part of the council or possessing knowledge of the machine. They also won't retain any aggression. Additionally, they will be relocated to another part of Glob."

After leaving the court, Kurel asked if Lars and Collings would be willing to visit the neighboring planet with him and an ambassador to offer an apology.

Later, Lars asked Collings if he was interested in joining. Collings readily agreed

THE JOURNEY TO THE OTHER PLANET

Lars and Collings prepared to travel to the other planet. They brought along the prisoners who had been caught in the act. The idea was that they would help the group integrate into their world, which the prisoners called Proxi.

The journey to Proxi took thirteen days, and they arrived in orbit above the planet. They contacted air traffic control via radio and handed the microphone to the former prisoners. These individuals explained that two representatives from Glob and two from a planet called Earth were making a diplomatic visit and wished to meet with the planet's leadership. They received clearance to land and were guided to the appropriate landing site.

As they stepped out of the ship, they saw thousands of people gathered as spectators. Close to the ship stood three soldiers, sharply dressed. The man and woman who led the way saluted by placing their hands on their hearts. They shook hands with the military officers, and the crowd erupted in cheers. When the others stepped forward, the men gave a slight nod of the head. Translators were turned on. Kurel greeted them and thanked them for receiving the delegation.

"Follow me," said one of the soldiers curtly. They were led to a vehicle with ten seats. Everyone boarded, and an armed guard sat next to the driver. They drove to a large palace and followed the soldiers inside, with the guard trailing behind.

They sat around a large table where more people in formal attire were seated. Each place was set with a glass and a bottle.

"Welcome to Proxi! As you understand, we are somewhat suspicious of you after the events of the past few years. We've received some explanations from our honored pilots who were in your custody. You may now present your case, and we promise to listen."

Kurel cleared his throat and said, "Honored leaders, I am the chairman of the council on the planet Glob, and I am here to apologize for the bombings you have suffered. That was never our intention; it was the work of evil individuals from our planet, acting without our knowledge. Those individuals have been punished and can never do harm again. Their goal was to seize power on our planet and attack all habitable planets nearby. If not for the help of these men from the planet Earth, located on the other side of space, we would not have uncovered the crimes of our own citizens. We are a peaceful people who do not practice violence, and as you may have noticed, we did not defend ourselves when you attacked us. If it pleases you, I would like the representatives from Earth to explain why they are here." He sat down.

Lars stood and said, "Honored leadership of the planet Proxi, as mentioned, we come from Earth, and we discovered a way to travel through space in search of life. Upon arriving at Glob, we found that life there was not so different from our own evolution. Our world has produced many things but has also polluted our atmosphere, leading to global warming and natural disasters. Our planet is only half the size of your two planets combined. We have learned that we must address our rapidly growing population, as our planet can no longer sustain everyone. Earth is overpopulated. We have an agreement with the leadership of Glob to relocate some people there, with the goal of living in harmony and promoting agriculture. We do not want to repeat the mistakes of the past by poisoning the atmosphere. It will take time, but our planet will heal. We had the equipment to fire weapons, but it was only intended for peacekeeping purposes. We have endured long periods of war between nations, and this opportunity has allowed us to unite and work together. We hope we can become friends and exchange knowledge. Thank you for your time!"

Several speakers from Proxi then spoke, expressing relief that the hostilities between the planets had finally ceased.

"We, too, do not wish for war, as we have ample space for our people and strive to live in harmony with nature. There is food for everyone, and we hope we can reach an agreement with both your worlds. We should sit down and work out a plan for the future. We will meet with our representatives and then return with a proposal."

"You are all welcome to a dinner where we can get to know each other better."

During the dinner, they were able to talk freely with their tablemates thanks to the translators they wore. The people of Proxi seemed peaceful and in many ways resembled the people of Earth. There was much laughter, and they enjoyed musical performances by both men and women. On Glob, they had not encountered many women; while there were female council members, the majority were men.

In the evening, the delegates were offered rooms, and they agreed to continue discussions the next day.

After a good night's sleep, they were served food and drinks that resembled coffee and tea. It tasted good, and no one fell ill from the food or drink. The next day, negotiations continued, and the atmosphere was significantly friendlier than during their first meeting at the airport. The representatives from Proxi explained that their planet also had a warm climate and dense jungles with both animals and various human tribes. There was no hostility between the tribes and the urban population, and they had a relatively small population in relation to the size of the planet.

After several days, they reached an agreement for an exchange between the planets Proxi and Glob, along with cooperation with representatives from Earth. According to the agreement, humans from Earth would also be allowed to settle on Proxi, and they were allocated an area almost as large as Earth itself. Glob would contribute its technological expertise. The technology for creating wormholes was discussed, but it was decided that the current construction would not be used. Instead, they would program the system so that travel could only occur between agreed-upon locations. They would also receive technology to detect unauthorized connections.

Collings announced that he would contact his planet later to see if they wanted to join the agreement. He expressed optimism that his world would welcome the proposal, but they would give a final response as soon as possible and then plan potential settlements on the new planets.

After spending two weeks on Proxi, they made the thirteen-day journey back to Glob. Upon arrival, Kurel presented the agreement between the planets to the council, which immediately approved the proposals.

Collings returned to Earth and informed all the presidents and leaders about the proposal, asking them to consider the possibilities of establishing settlements on the new planets. The leaders returned to their respective governments, and the media reported on the agreements and the opportunities they would bring for Earth's well-being.

As expected, all nations accepted the proposals and provided estimates of how many people would be willing to relocate. In every country, organizations were established to plan and assess who would have the opportunity to emigrate. Most of those who wished to emigrate came from India, China, and Europe. Everyone was informed that emigration would be permanent and that they could not expect to return.

In total, estimates were made of how many could emigrate. The first settlers would need knowledge of construction and nature care. Initially, an agricultural society would be established, as the climate was favorable for this. Regulations were also set on how to handle the local animals, and quotas were established for how much meat could be consumed. No animals or plants from Earth could be brought to avoid introducing invasive species. Everyone traveling to the new planets would pass through a gate that would kill any bacteria on equipment and clothing. They were reminded of how the Inca people had fared when the Spanish brought diseases that nearly wiped them out.

Livestock and horses would be allowed, but only the latest technology that did not harm the atmosphere could be used. Everyone had learned from the mistakes of the past.

THE NEW WORLDS

The migration was to begin with those in refugee camps, the poorest of the poor. Naturally, it would be voluntary, and they would be people eager to start fresh. It was agreed that connections would be made via the machine in each country for transport to various parts of Glob, according to the regions designated by the inhabitants there and in line with their promises.

Tools and everyday items that the new settlers would find useful had been gathered. They were to build a society based on their various cultures and needs. In practice, the land was divided into many new countries, where each could retain its own culture. For people coming from large cities, it was a bit more difficult to revert to a simpler lifestyle, but the key difference was that there was plenty of farmland rich in minerals and very fertile. The new settlements were provided with solar panels and technology from the inhabitants of Glob, producing clean energy without polluting the soil.

Upon arriving at their new locations, they were informed about the animals in the area, which ones were dangerous, and which were edible. They were also told about the plants that grew there and which had healing properties. There were no snakes on Glob, but various types of lizards existed. These lizards were large but not dangerous to humans, as long as they weren't threatened when guarding their young. In the seas and large lakes, there was an abundance of marine life, including fish, crabs, and whales. All these creatures were very large, thanks to the plentiful and nutrient-rich food supply.

Nearly a third of Earth's population wanted to emigrate, and many chose the planet Proxi because its inhabitants resembled humans more than those on Glob.

As more people emigrated, pressure on Earth decreased, and the land was better distributed for those who remained. Emissions dropped, and societies and technologies developed in a sustainable way. Many families were split since not everyone wanted to emigrate, but people respected those who chose to move, as it was their own decision.

Despite so many having moved to the new planets, settlements were still sparse, and they didn't meet often due to the large distances between them. In some places, cities were built, while in others, settlements were spread across vast areas. There was plenty of space, and they could live off the land.

Initially, they had problems with animals, which were only active at night. Some people had died in attacks by these creatures. However, they learned to protect themselves by always having lights, which scared off the animals, as they were afraid of the light.

A council had been formed to oversee and ensure that no violations occurred and to make decisions about laws that had been agreed upon. There were individuals who tried to steal or take over others' land, but the laws ensured that these people were punished. However, this happened rarely, as there was food for everyone. Trade gradually increased, as different cultures were skilled in crafting useful items. There was no currency yet, only bartering.

Many diseases that had existed on Earth could be cured here, thanks to the knowledge of diseases developed on Glob and Proxi, which were far more advanced than Earth's.

ISOLATION

After ten years, the authorities on Glob and Lars began to notice that the connections were becoming increasingly unreliable. The scientists on Glob and Lars didn't know the cause. It seemed as though the machines were becoming more and more exhausted, even though new machines were being built. The decline in functionality suggested that the technology would cease to work within a few months. It was as if space itself had become saturated with manipulation. Soon, it would be impossible to maintain contact with Earth. The scientists and those who had established and organized the settlements had to decide where they belonged. This also applied to Lars and Collings, who faced a difficult choice as they had been able to switch between Earth and the planets.

The machines still worked flawlessly on the planets. This was useful when they needed to travel between different populated areas. They prepared Earth's population for the likelihood that contact would soon be severed. On Earth, however, the Mars project continued to make progress. A small city had been built under a large dome, which had been developed to be completely radiation-proof.

They had also developed space rockets capable of reaching farther and faster, though not as far as Glob or Proxi. The distances to these planets were enormous. Despite this, exploration of the Milky Way continued on Earth, and they hadn't given up hope of finding life within the reachable regions.

Earth had already begun to heal; the average temperature had dropped by two degrees, and the polar regions were rebuilding with ice. They had achieved zero carbon emissions, and there were no more vehicles powered by gasoline or diesel. Over the years, nearly half of Earth's population had emigrated to the planets. For the first time in human history, there was peace everywhere. The cooperation around emigration had strengthened collaboration between countries, and poverty had almost been eradicated, except in a few areas of the world. No one was starving anymore!

Lately, Lars had become acquainted with a woman on the planet Proxi, and their relationship had developed into a deep love. Lars had often wondered whether it would be possible for them to have children together, given that they came from entirely different worlds. But they never openly discussed these matters. The woman, who was a little younger than him, was named Marja. In Lars' view, she was a very beautiful and wise woman. He could hardly believe that such a beautiful woman wanted to be with him. They truly enjoyed each other's company and were both eager to explore the parts of the planet that were still unknown.

Proxi was very similar to Glob in its development, and in many areas, the animal and plant life had evolved in fascinating ways. The planets were truly twin planets. The primary differences were in the appearance and physiology of their inhabitants. For this reason, they wanted to investigate life on Proxi. Marja had always wanted to explore the areas that remained undiscovered. One journey they took together was to the jungle, where it was rumored that there were people of some kind. They ventured into the jungle but were very cautious and alert to avoid being attacked by wild animals. Both carried a pistol loaded with fast-acting tranquilizers in case they needed to defend themselves. They also brought powerful flashlights in case they got caught after dark and needed to protect themselves from predators, like those they had previously encountered on Glob, which were highly sensitive to light.

By now, Lars had learned the languages of both Proxi and Glob and could speak fluently with Marja without any difficulty. After hiking in the jungle for a few days, they reached a small hilltop and could see smoke rising from a valley below. Slowly, they approached the source of the smoke and heard sounds of people, though they couldn't make out what was being said. Suddenly, three men and a woman appeared behind them, threatening them with spears. Lars and Marja raised their hands to show they meant no harm. The strangers gestured for them to move toward the place where the voices were coming from.

Pushing through the underbrush, they emerged to find a group of people who looked just like they were from Earth. They were dressed in leather clothing adorned with beautiful decorations. They looked well-nourished and healthy. As Lars and Marja stepped out of the brush, the people gasped in surprise until they saw the men and women who had captured them. The newcomers looked at Lars and Marja curiously, without any visible aggression. Lars and Marja stopped in front of them and placed their hands over their hearts as a greeting. Some of them returned the gesture in the same way. They began to speak to Lars and Marja, but the pair didn't understand the language. Lars responded in his own language, indicating that they didn't understand, to make it clear they spoke different tongues.

An elderly man stepped forward and said, "They don't understand the old language. It's been a long time since anyone spoke the Proxi language. What brings you here?"

Lars responded in Proxi: "My name is Lars, and this is Marja. We wanted to explore the jungle, as it seemed unknown to the people of Proxi."

Marja added, "We mean no harm, we were just curious because we had heard there were people living here whom no one had met. We thought it was just a myth."

The old man replied, "We have not mingled with the people outside the jungle. Many years ago, we met a man at the edge of the forest. We traded a little with him, and I learned his language. We are a peaceful people, living off what the forest provides. You are welcome to visit our village if you wish."

He turned to his people and spoke to them for a moment in their language. Many of them nodded and looked happy and friendly. Lars and Marja nodded in return and told the old man they would be happy to visit their village.

He waved for them to follow. After about an hour's walk, they arrived at a small village with around twenty log houses. When they arrived, the villagers were very curious about the two strangers, partly because Marja looked different with her slightly larger head, and partly because of Lars' light skin. The people in the village were dark-skinned, resembling South Americans. There were large carts on wheels, and in a pen, there were several animals of the type Lars had seen in a video, where one such animal attacked and overturned a car during one of the first expeditions on Glob.

Lars asked the old man if the animals weren't dangerous and recounted the story of when such a creature had attacked the car. The old man replied that they were not aggressive and could be easily trained as draft animals. He explained that some had become feral and were afraid, especially if they had calves. They had kept these animals for hundreds of years and lived side by side in mutual dependence. The animals were strong and helped with pulling down trees and transporting them, while the people farmed the land and grew a type of grass that the animals liked very much.

Lars asked why they didn't live with the other people on the planet. The old man explained that they actually lived much farther away by a sea on the other side of the jungle and that they were here to gather special plants and roots that they used as medicine. Marja mentioned that the people of Proxi weren't as interested in exploration and had developed in their own part of the planet. They knew that evolution had produced different human races, but since they rarely met, they weren't very interested in each other. Marja mentioned that she, personally, was curious and researched the different races found in other regions. That was why she and Lars were there, to expand their knowledge. Apart from the difference in skin color, Lars and the native people were very similar. They stayed in the village for several weeks and found the people to be friendly, cheerful, and skilled hunters.

The villagers offered Marja and Lars the chance to accompany them back to their cities by the sea to deliver and sell the medicinal plants. The old man mentioned that the plants were highly sought after and brought good payment. Marja was very interested and asked Lars if they should go along. Lars felt it was obvious they should join, and they were in no hurry to return home. The journey would be long, but not particularly challenging, as the animals would pull the carts, and their size would deter any predators.

THE JOURNEY WESTWARD

The villagers packed the carts with sacks and household items from the cottages, fastening the beasts of burden to the carts. The carts were so tall that they were equivalent to about two stories. The lower part was used for sleeping, while the upper part was intended for sitting and enjoying the surroundings. They followed a forest path that had clearly been used for many years. Occasionally, large plains and lakes opened up before them. They stopped at one of the lakes and fished with nets. Each throw of the net resulted in it being filled with fish when pulled up. They cooked the fresh fish and served it with a type of potato. The flavor was fantastic, with spices perfectly suited to Lars' taste. Leftover fish was preserved in brine, and some were hung up under the roof to dry. During the journey, they saw many different animals and birds. At times, the sound of birds and other creatures was deafening. Once, when passing a clearing in the jungle, they saw a number of humanoid apes gathering fruits in the trees. They were shy and quickly disappeared when they saw the caravan.

After traveling for a month, they said it was about a week until they would reach the first city. During the journey, Marja and Lars had learned much of the local language and could now converse with the other people without problems. Everyone was friendly and jovial, and they had many laughs along the way when they mispronounced words, leading to amusing misunderstandings. The women sometimes blushed when they made language mistakes.

However, Marja had been feeling unwell for the past few days, experiencing nausea and general fatigue. She complained about the rocking of the cart. The old man examined her and said there was no danger but suggested they see a doctor when they arrived in the city.

As the jungle began to thin out, they traveled across meadows with grass and scattered trees, laden with an abundance of fruit. They tasted the fruit, which was sweet and juicy, similar to peaches. On the horizon, tall towers and a large city by the water could be seen. As they rolled into the city's streets, they were met by a large crowd welcoming them. Word had spread that a man and a woman from another land had arrived. The cart stopped at a low building, and Lars tried to read the text on the door. He could make out the word "hospital." The old man asked them to come inside.

Inside the hospital, they were greeted by a man wearing glasses who welcomed them. He asked Marja to lie down on a soft bed. The old man explained that Marja had been feeling nauseous and occasionally vomited, especially in the mornings. The doctor listened, felt her stomach, and examined her mouth. After washing his hands, he said, "You have a serious condition." Marja became alarmed. The doctor continued, "You have a very common human condition," he said, smiling. "You're pregnant! Congratulations!"

Marja was shocked and said, "Is that true? I didn't think we could have children because we come from different races." The doctor replied, "You and we share the same basic genetic makeup, and the differences are mostly in appearance." Marja's face lit up with a huge smile, and she looked at Lars, who was equally overjoyed and surprised. Lars said, "I'm so happy! I've always wanted to have a child. Are you happy?" he asked Marja. She replied, "I'm thrilled to be having a child with you."

The doctor explained that it was early in the pregnancy and that Marja could continue her daily life as usual. Soon, the nausea would subside. Once she learned about her condition, her anxiety lifted, and she beamed with happiness. For Lars, this was the greatest joy he had ever experienced. There was no doubt that he would stay on Proxi.

They were given accommodation in a modern apartment with both water and electricity. Lars asked how the electricity was generated and if it had any emissions. He was told the electricity came from a fusion power plant with no emissions. They didn't have vehicles or large machines; the carts were sufficient for transport. They traded goods with other cities by the sea, which had large ships for transporting goods and people. Outside the city, there were enormous farms producing food and fodder for their animals, which resembled pigs, cows, chickens, and horses. The lush landscape, with an average temperature of twenty-seven degrees Celsius year-round, allowed for multiple growing seasons. The people possessed great technical knowledge, primarily used to provide water and conveniences in the cities. Maps that Marja had shown that the sea stretched around the entire planet, and the winds there were fairly constant. They had developed boats that could sail long distances, but they had no need for them. The people were content with their way of life.

Lars and Marja were invited to a welcome feast at the town hall. They were offered a change of clothes at a place resembling a department store. There were many beautiful clothes to choose from, all free of charge. Marja chose a stunning dress with bright colors and fine embroidery, while Lars selected a shirt and trousers with patterns on the shirt. When he looked at himself in the mirror, he was satisfied and thought he looked younger.

At the town hall, they were greeted by many people dressed in colorful outfits. The old man welcomed them and led them to a large table where they were invited to sit. After everyone had sat down, several people came up on a stage and played instruments Lars had never seen before. The music was soft and harmonious, evoking feelings of security and happiness. After they finished playing, there was strong applause. The old man got up on stage, cleared his throat, and said:

"We want to welcome Lars and Marja to this celebration and to our world. It's rare that we have visitors from other lands, and it has been a delightful acquaintance during the weeks we've spent together. Lars has played a significant role in uniting our planet with our neighboring planet. His efforts have contributed to peace and security, and now a major milestone has been reached with Marja's pregnancy, as she will give birth to a child that is a blend of two races, enriching our world. Welcome!"

As the old man spoke, the guests at the table applauded. At the same time, Marja, feeling shy, looked down. After the speech, food and drink were served. Most of the food was vegetarian, with a small portion resembling meat. Lars asked his neighbor what the meat was, and he was told it came from large sea creatures, similar to whale meat. The vegetables came from the farms outside the city. The drink was somewhat fermented, resembling beer, while Marja received a different drink that looked like juice. The server mentioned that the fermented drink wasn't good for her baby.

THE JOURNEY HOME

After spending a month in the city and its surroundings, both Marja and Lars began to feel a bit restless. Marja longed to return home to share the wonderful news of their upcoming child. Lars, who still felt butterflies every time he looked at Marja, was overjoyed and deeply in love. Whenever he had the chance, he gave her a long hug and kissed her. The people in the city seemed surprised by his public displays of affection. Lars wondered why.

The old man explained, "Our people find it difficult to show emotions publicly. While it's allowed, it's not customary to express feelings in public places. We are an open and happy people, but public kissing is still uncommon. Our society is traditional and holds on to certain old customs, although it's becoming more common with time. Many who work at sea are away from their families for months, and those who remain don't want to remind them of the separation they feel," the old man explained.

As they prepared to head home, they said goodbye to the friends they had made, especially the old man, who had taught them so much about the city's people and customs. They saw him as a wise and modern person with a big heart. They promised to return someday.

They arranged to sail on a merchant ship to the outermost city by the sea, closer to Marja's hometown. From there, they would be able to join expeditions that collected medicinal plants.

Lars was looking forward to arriving there, as he had built a villa outside the city. Having chosen not to remain on Earth, he had sold his homes in Sweden and Houston, earning a significant sum. During his time at the Space Center, he had also made good money, and with few expenses, he had been able to buy a lot of equipment through the machine when it still worked. He had purchased a large number of solar panels and electric motors, as well as a building he filled with equipment. He also acquired four jeeps that could be charged by solar panels. Much of what he bought could be exchanged for local currency, giving him a solid start to support both himself and his future family.

The journey aboard the merchant ship went smoothly, with calm waves and a favorable wind. They sailed along the coast, surrounded by beautiful scenery. During the voyage, they stopped in a few cities to load and unload goods. Eventually, they reached the outermost city and disembarked. The trip had been smooth for Marja, who was now free from nausea. A small bump on her belly clearly showed she was pregnant, and she often gently touched it with a happy smile.

The captain of the merchant ship helped them join an expedition that would take them further toward Marja's hometown. The expedition included boats with carts and draft animals, as well as a small sailboat that Lars and Marja would use for the final stretch. During the journey, they saw large whales swimming near the boats, along with many other large fish and animals resembling seals and dolphins. Huge birds circled above them, diving into the sea and emerging with large fish in their talons.

Lars spent much time studying the ocean and pondering the planets. He wondered how life could develop so similarly on both this planet and Earth. He speculated that planets with oxygen and a temperate environment close to their sun might have similar conditions for life, leading to comparable evolutionary patterns. He reflected on how human races had evolved independently on Earth and found evidence that evolution here had also led to different human development stages, from the great apes to the people they were now traveling with.

When they reached the point where the expedition would continue into the jungle, the sailboat was loaded and launched. They boarded with supplies of food and water for the journey. Marja, who had some sailing experience, received instructions on how to handle the boat.

They said goodbye to the crew and hoisted the sails, continuing along the coast. With good winds, they neared Marja's hometown. As they got closer, they encountered more ships and boats. They steered into a harbor Marja recognized and moored the boat at a dock. They carried the gifts they had received from the fishing people inside, took a shared shower, and washed each other's backs. They enjoyed being together in their own home. Lars gently caressed Marja's belly and said he was the happiest man in the world.

As they relaxed on the sofa, they felt the strain of the journey and decided to go to bed, sleeping closely together. Lars woke up early the next morning, catching the aroma of coffee, which he had brought with him from Earth. He had received permission to bring coffee beans to plant his own coffee bushes. When he got up, Marja had prepared breakfast and greeted him with a hug and kiss. They ate together, reminiscing about their travels. Marja looked over her notes, which she had written throughout the journey, and planned to write a book about her experiences.

They were now preparing to meet Marja's parents and siblings. Lars was nervous about how they would react when they shared the news about the upcoming baby. Marja reassured him, saying they would be thrilled to become grandparents for the first time.

In the middle of the day, they set off in one of the jeeps and drove to Marja's parents' home. People along the road looked curiously as they passed, but they had seen Lars driving before.

Marja opened the door and called out, "Hello!" Her mother and father rushed forward to embrace her. They expressed their concern over not having heard from them for a long time. Marja assured them that everything had gone well and gave a brief summary of their travels and experiences.

They were soon seated at the table, served coffee and soup. Marja's siblings also came home and were happy to see them. After some time, Marja said, "We have some news to share with you."

She paused dramatically and looked at her parents.

"You're going to be grandparents! I'm expecting a baby, and it's due in three months."

Her mother, father, and siblings were completely shocked. Her father stammered, "But… how did this happen?"

Marja replied, "The same way it always happens, of course."

Her father continued, "I understand that, but how is it possible? You're from different worlds. Is it really possible?"

Lars spoke up, "Thank you for being certain I'm the father! It turns out that we're compatible despite our different races. I'm so happy to have a child with your daughter, whom I love with all my heart!"

Once the initial shock wore off, everyone around the table congratulated them, expressing their joy over the new family member. Marja's mother reached out, placed her hand on Marja's belly, and said, "It's time for you to pledge your fidelity to each other for life. You must do this through a ceremony."

"Of course," Lars agreed.

THE CEREMONY

The preparations for the ceremony were extensive, with family members being invited according to tradition. The woman's parents always handled the planning, and the news that an Earthling and a person from Proxi were having a child together made it particularly significant. Some Earthlings who had moved to Proxi contacted Lars to congratulate him. They expressed how reassuring it was to know they could have children with the people of Proxi if they met someone they liked, and that this made them feel fully integrated into society.

A few days before the ceremony, Lars received a visit from a Proxian who knocked on his door. Lars opened it, and the man asked if Lars would consider a proposal he had. Lars recognized him from the electronics store where he had shopped. The man's name was Dodo.

Lars invited Dodo inside and asked if he wanted a cup of coffee. Dodo replied that he had never tasted coffee but had heard that it was a drink Earthlings enjoyed. He accepted and said he would love to try it.

Dodo sipped the coffee, looking pleased, and said he liked the taste.

"You wanted to ask me something?" Lars inquired.

"Yes, exactly," Dodo answered. "I've seen you driving a vehicle, which I believe is called a car. I would like to manufacture something like it. Do you know how the technology works?"

"Not exactly," Lars replied. "There's a battery that stores power from solar panels and drives an electric motor. I don't know much more, but I do have a few extra cars you can borrow if you'd like to try figuring it out yourself. There's a manual with diagrams of the parts that might help. Since you have the technology to build rockets, you should have the ability to manufacture engines and other control systems."

"Can I really borrow a car?"

"Yes, of course. I can show you how to drive it if you come with me," Lars responded.

They went to the storage building, and Lars backed out one of the cars. He showed Dodo the controls, how to brake, and how to accelerate. Dodo sat in the driver's seat and drove a short distance. Lars said, "Drive it and let me know how it goes."

"Thank you," said Dodo as he drove away.

Lars wondered if Dodo would be able to figure out how the car worked and whether he could manufacture a similar one. Time would tell!

The day of the ceremony arrived, and Lars and Marja headed to the venue where it would take place. They were greeted by Marja's parents, who welcomed them warmly. The venue was full of people, some of whom Lars recognized. Most were new faces, and he didn't know their familial ties. Lars was surprised to see two couples standing by a wall – emigrants from the midlands of Sweden! He approached them cheerfully.

"How did you end up here? Did you know we had a ceremony today?" Lars asked.

"We were invited by your wife's mother, who knew we were from Sweden," one of the women replied.

"I'm really glad to see you here; you're very welcome."

"We wouldn't miss it. You're quite a celebrity here. And by the way, congratulations on the baby! It's wonderful news. Perhaps our future children will find a partner among the Proxians, and our families can unite."

Lars went to Marja's mother and thanked her for inviting his fellow countrymen. She explained that they knew these couples and that they had become well-known for being hardworking and well-adjusted to Proxi's culture.

A bell rang, and Marja's father stepped onto the stage. He cleared his throat and began to speak:

"I welcome you all to this ceremony, which will unite Marja and Lars as partners for life. Come up here, Marja and Lars. You have begun your journey together, and we all see your love for each other. You are now to promise to stay together for the future generations, uniting us all no matter where we come from."

He gestured to Marja, who stepped forward and said,

"According to our customs, I vow to be faithful and love my husband for all the years from now until death separates us."

Lars stood before her and said,

"According to your customs and the customs we have on Earth, I vow to you, Marja, to be faithful, support, and love you until death separates us."

The crowd in the hall applauded and cheered.

After the ceremony, everyone sat down at the tables and enjoyed the various dishes that were served. Once the meal was over, Marja's father surprised everyone by going around and offering coffee. He had secretly taken the coffee beans from Lars and Marja's house without them knowing. He had watched Lars brew coffee many times when they were guests at their home. Almost everyone accepted the drink they had heard so much about.

Later in the evening, people began dancing and performing for each other. The celebration lasted for several hours, becoming a bit tiring for Marja, who, after all, was pregnant. Both Lars and Marja thanked everyone for attending the ceremony and wished them a good night!

DEVELOPMENT

Marja had given birth to their child, a girl. It was clear that she had inherited features from both parents: fair skin and a slightly larger head, though not as large as the heads of the native children.

Dodo came by and returned the car. He reported that he had managed to manufacture cars, though they were not as advanced as Lars' vehicle. He had used a different technology and developed a battery that was twice as efficient. He thanked Lars for letting him borrow the car and came with a proposal.

"I'd like you to become my partner and co-owner. I know you need something to do, and with your wife and child, it's good to have an income source," Dodo said.

"It's an enticing offer. I've actually been considering a product that I believe could improve transportation. I would like to develop larger engines that can drive ships and operate without emissions. Could this be something we could invest in?" Lars asked.

"That would be a perfect product, and I think there's demand for both large and smaller boats. With my new battery, we can create powerful engines," Dodo replied.

"I have some knowledge about developing propellers that work in water. I also have contacts with a people who primarily engage in maritime activities and fishing. I believe they would be interested," Lars said.

They agreed that Lars would visit Dodo to discuss various ventures and how their collaboration might look. They also considered the possibility of developing solar panels locally, as it was important to be able to charge the batteries to keep the system functioning.

Their collaboration on cars and engines proved to be successful. There was significant interest in buying cars and equipping ships with engines and propellers. As developers, they earned good income, and all production was carried out in an environmentally friendly way with no emissions. Their success was so substantial that they even began exporting to Glob!